END OF EARTH, BOOK 3

MATT SIMONS

CHAPTER 1

BROKEN

"WHAT AM I NOW?"

The collective memories of many failed lives. Fading away as I slowly decay into nothing. This brain tumor slowly grows. It doesn't hurt, nothing does any more. Pain has left this body after treatment began. Being pumped full of poison as they fed me pain meds that only make me feel sick. Only delayed the inevitable, I wish my death could be simple. I have to live out my sentence. The State of Arizona sentenced me to five years with three more added on for additional violations, and I will see this sentence to the end no matter the quality of my life.

I was Lieutenant Jason Baker of the United States Army infantry. I fought on the front lines of the Third World War while all of my friends died. Then in a flash of a light from a nuclear bomb, my mind was sent back into my eleven year old body. The war changed me too much to be home. When my childhood bullies confronted me, I fought back as if I was still in the war, putting five kids in the hospital with broken and disfigured bodies. Maybe I deserve this death for all the violence I have committed. The warden says, "I don't belong in civilized society." I'm just a monster.

The only light in my dying days is Angel. I entrusted the secrets of time travel to him. I knew it as soon as he stopped the war. When he took my notebook full of equations, I lost my connection to the nuclear explosion. That means the timeline shifted enough to remove the nuke from the future. Now with the war prevented, this timeline no longer needs me.

"Thank you, Angel."

Now all I can do is wait for the darkness of the void to take me. Strapped to this hospital bed, alone in the juvey infirmary, I have nothing to pass the time but my thoughts. It's somehow worse than being locked in solitary confinement. At least there I could freely walk around, filling the time with calisthenics. Now I get one hour of supervised exercise that is essentially me limping around this bland room of faded white brick walls. I don't even get to go outside anymore because I'm too dangerous, apparently.

For fucks sake, the left side of my body is partially paralyzed after my stroke, so I ain't that much of a danger anymore. Now I may have injected another inmate with my chemo medication, but that was to protect my friend. I was in no condition for a physical fight. All the muscles I built have decayed. I am now a bald and pale white skin draped on a skeleton. And I did try to strangle the nurse with my IV tube last week. In my defense, she snuck up on me. I thought she was an enemy. The medical staff will avoid me for a while after one of my outbursts, leaving me to fester until my stink becomes unbearable. Even on the bad days,

I can't tell the difference between what's real and the war in my head.

I can barely see anything as my eyesight decays, covering my world with a thickening haze. I've been staring at what I think is the ceiling fan for days, but it's so blurry I can't make out the blades no matter how hard I try to focus. It just looks like a spinning disk.

Trapped here with nothing but my tainted memories, I try to remember the good times before the war. My favorite memory is the last time I was with all my friends as we shared our first drink of alcohol on the mountain, overlooking Yuma. Zack called it Snake bite, that silver-haired comic. He died with Alex, a six-foot, six-inch giant on a Navy ship in the North Atlantic, while fighting the Russians.

My best friend Rick joined the army after I was drafted. I try to picture him laughing before everything shifts to his final moments, gasping for air as his lungs fill with blood. Can't remember his normal face anymore. All I see are his blood burst eyes from the chemical weapons. I remember how his hand grew limp as he coughed up blood.

"I couldn't save him."

I can feel water forming at the edge of my eyes. No, I will not cry. I saved them in this life. I stopped the war. Angel saved us all.

Angel was meant to die from blood loss on the other side of the world, in a war we didn't ask for. The world war was meant to begin 12/20/2012, but that day has passed and the missiles never flew.

"I am no longer needed. Thank you, Angel," I whisper to myself, waiting for this painful existence to end.

"Happy new year, Jason," says someone above the bed.

I wipe my eyes with my sleeve, trying to clear my vision. "Is it happy?"

Luis says, "It's a new year. A time for new beginnings."

Recognizing his voice, I say, "Or ends."

I can feel Luis standing beside me. He's a lanky Hispanic delinquent. His baggy clothes make him look bigger than he really is. He uses the illusion to avoid confrontations, for he's not a fighter in this life. He faces a long prison sentence from making friends with the wrong crowd. During a carjacking his friend got shot and killed, adding a homicide charge to his sentence. He still has nine years left before the possibility of parole.

He tries to see me as often as possible, believing he owes me a debt for protecting him on his first day in Juvey. He is no longer my responsibility. Another delinquent I saved after being stabbed, David and his gang protect Luis now.

Luis takes the seat next to my bed. "So, are you going to watch the Times Square ball drop? That's the only thing they're letting us watch in B block."

I keep my eyes pointed up at the ceiling, focusing on the spinning fan and then looking past it, still trying to focus my failing eyesight. "The nurses took away my TV privileges. They say it's causing my delusions to grow out of control."

"Do you think it is?"

"Maybe… I'm not getting better." I turn to look at Luis, seeing a clear image of Luis's caved in face. His broken corpse from the war, filled in by memory where my sight has failed me. The blood drips from his body, pooling into the building's debris with all the other slain squad members. My hand remembers the pain of being mutilated by the explosion, so I look down, finding my hand still there, all in one piece. I squeeze my fingers as tight as I can but barely make a fist. "Medicine can't fix me anymore."

Luis sits quietly, lost for words.

Trying my best to keep the conversation going, I ask, "Are you ready for the transfer?"

"Of course I am. I've been following your training. I'll be running the adult prison in no time." Luis rolls up his sleeve to show off his muscles.

I hear through his fake confidence. "You don't have to act tough around me. Fear is natural—you just have to use it. Remember not to back down. The only value the inmates care about is strength. Prove it, then don't cause extra trouble. Last thing you want is to serve more time. Get out, and *live*. That's something I'll never get to do."

"Easy for you to say. Your transfer will be from one hospital room to another. You ain't gotta deal with the real shit in prison anymore."

"I've seen plenty of real shit."

His broken corpse of the past stares back at me with an inquisitorial look.

I say, "If you have a question, just ask. I can't read your mind."

He asks, "Are you really from the future? Like, can you prove it?"

I let the silence grow until the soft buzz of the overhead fan consumed it. Not quite winter yet, it's still hot. Finally, I say, "I can't. The future I know doesn't exist anymore. The missiles that were meant to destroy Hawaii weren't fired. All the friends I watched die, now live. This isn't my world. I am the collective memories of many Jasons all thrown back to this moment. My original worlds are still fighting, but there is nothing more I can do for them. Maybe when I die, I can go back to them or perhaps they will simply all fade away with me."

Luis looks at me with skepticism before finally speaking. "You spend too much time in your own head. I think you need a hobby."

"I am open to suggestions, but I can't see very well anymore, so reading's out. My grip is weak, so I can't work on anything. Plus, my restraints." With my good arm, I pull against the straps to show how little movement I have. "There's not a whole lot I can do anymore."

Luis says, "I could get you something to listen to. There's some old CDs in the library here, and I can lend you my CD player."

I agree, knowing Luis is just looking for an excuse to not spend time in the yard. Besides him, my visitors are few. Nurse Sheshna will check my vitals in the morning, at the start of her shift, and at the end of her shift in the evening. My food mostly consists of soup, delivered quickly and without conversation. She keeps her distance after a few of my violent nightmares. Thankfully the resident doctor has been here to pull me off. That is the only time I can remember even seeing a doctor.

My family visits every Sunday. Mom and Dad hold a brave face, but my slow death is destroying them. My older brother Pete acts like nothing has changed, still making jokes, while my sister Ann has broken down in tears during each visit.

"I wish I had just died in the desert. Things would have been easier."

CHAPTER 2

AT MIDNIGHT OF AN INMATE's eighteenth birthday, they are moved from the juvenile section of a prison to the adult section. This is the law for every prison in the United States. Even though I am a terminal inmate, Today I am being moved from the juvenile detention center on the outskirts of Phoenix, Arizona to the adult prison in Florence and kept separate for the adult inmate population until I turn eighteen. The law is the law.

I am transferred in an ambulance with a correction's officer and a paramedic. I can tell by their voices that the corrections officer is a man and the paramedic is a woman. Sleep would make the trip shorter, but my head feel too dizzy to get more than short bits of unconsciousness. It is kind of nice being outside the walls of Juvey. I try to keep my focus on the window at the back of the vehicle, seeing the bright light of the sun and feeling in on my skin as the other occupants make small talk.

The drive reminds me of Cairo. The loop out to the oil

fields and the drive back to post. The pointless monotony of it all.

The vehicle hits a small bump. I can clearly see yellow mist starts flowing in.

I shout, "Gas! Masks on!" *I need to find my gas mask.* "It's not here!" *We have to get out of the city as fast as possible. Rick doesn't have a mask either.* "Floor it! Now!" I yell as I thrash in the stretcher.

The paramedic reaches out to me, but the corrections officer stops her. "Don't mind him. He'll tire himself out soon."

She ignores his warning. Speaking softly, "It's okay. Everything is alright." She places her hands gently on my shoulders to stop me from moving.

I can only see an adversary preventing me from surviving the gas attack, so I try to swing my arms to fight back but only pull against the restraints. I change tactics and bite the arm on my shoulder. She lets out a slight yelp, pulling back before I can do any real damage.

The corrections officer says, "I warned you."

The paramedic says, "Crazy little fucker," as she takes out an alcohol wipe to clean the bitten area. "What's wrong with him? I was only told he was terminal."

I keep thrashing about, kicking my legs and straining my arms.

The corrections officer says, "Well, he's crazy. Fights like a bat out of hell. I watched that kid get into a fight on his first day in the clink five years ago. He challenged the top dogs on the lot. This little nutcase was willing to fight to the last breath. We had to pull him away for his own safety."

The paramedic says, "Poor kid."

"Don't pity him. He was convicted of Aggravated Assault on five other kids. Left them disfigured in the hospital."

"What's he terminal with?"

"Brain tumor, apparently."

The paramedic finishes bandaging her arm. "He has a terminal brain tumor and is prone to violence? Did no one consider those might be connected? The poor child is clearly suffering."

The corrections officer shrugs his shoulders and leans back in his seat. "He's still a danger to society. If it were up to me, we would've just taken him out to the desert and left him with the wild animals."

The offended paramedic says, "Well, it's a good thing that it's not up to you."

Eventually my body gives out, going limp in the bed as I suck in the yellow air, expecting it to kill me. My head aches as I finally start to drift into a partial sleep.

At the entrance to Florence prison, two men in black suits with dark sunglasses stand with my new warden.

The corrections officer greets the warden with a firm handshake. "You must be Ron Credio. I have your new inmate. Heads up, he's a handful." He gestures to the paramedic with her fresh bandage as she pushes my stretcher out of the vehicle. The corrections officer then asks, "Are those the new uniforms around here? They look expensive." He points to the men in suits. "Fancy, but it must get hot in the summer."

Warden Credio says, "Don't mind them. Here's the paperwork." He hands over a folder of signed papers. "That will be all."

As the paramedic pushes me to the front gate of the

prison, I feel a new source of danger when one the Men in Black stops her. His voice is deep and clear, "We'll take it from here, ma'am."

As he grasps the stretcher at the foot end, the other silently moves directly behind her. His massive frame over-shadows the small woman. She starts to argue that she wants her stretcher back. The silent one reaches into his coat. The paramedic senses danger and jumps away, then she sees he only holds a small envelope.

"This should cover the price, ma'am."

I feel as though I can hear the paramedic's heart racing. She takes the envelope and hurries back to the ambulance, never taking her eyes off the men.

The corrections officer hops into the vehicle next to her. As he closes the door he says, "What a bunch of creeps."

The paramedic opens the envelope to see it filled with hundred-dollar bills, at least five thousand dollars' worth. She yells to the driver, "Lue, get us out of here!"

Lue, who has been playing imaginary drums to his music, doesn't hear her.

"Let's go!" she screams, now more unhinged.

Lue jolts back to reality, turns on the engine and speeds away.

The corrections officer asks, "Are you alright?"

The paramedic says, "The further from those guys, the better I'll be. I honestly thought they were going…" She looks down at the envelope of cash in her lap.

"Going to what?"

"Never mind."

The men in black suits take me to a white van with a government license plate. I try to ask what is happening, but my body isn't responding to my thoughts. One of the men hands Warden Credio a black briefcase.

Warden Credio thanks the man, but he doesn't let go. "Remember, the prisoner died in transport."

Warden Credio says, "Indeed he did. It's such a tragedy, isn't it?"

The man lets go of the briefcase, allowing Warden Credio to open it and see the stacks of money inside. He closes it. "It has been an honor working with you gentlemen, as always."

How can I hear all of this? I can't see but it's all clear as day.

Weakly fighting against my restraints again, I finally let out, "But I'm not dead! Who are you people!"

The van doors close. I try to break free of my restraints until a needle is inserted into my IV line.

I try to scream, "Let me go!" as darkness takes me.

CHAPTER 3

JOHNATHAN KANE

"**J**UST PICK A CHANNEL ALREADY, John. You've already scrolled through everything twice," says my current roommate. Todd is one of the few survivors of my brother's mass shooting on post. Barry tried to finish off everyone, but Lieutenant Todd got lucky, only getting hit in the leg when Barry opened fire on the parking lot crowd. I'll never admit this out loud, but Barry was the best shot out of us three brothers.

I ignore my roommate and continue flipping through the many channels on this small hospital TV. I honestly don't know what I'm even looking for anymore. Maybe I just want to feel the numb discomfort in my hand pressing the buttons.

"Go back! The food network was playing *Master Chief*. They were cooking meat drizzled in barbeque sauce on an open flame." He's licking his lips in lust.

I would like to tell him to shut up, but my ability to talk is hindered after Barry ripped my cheek open. My tongue keeps licking the stitches, sending little bouts of pain through my mouth.

I stop on a channel playing commercials for life insurance.

"Just give me the remote, Captain."

Through gritted teeth, I growl from the back of my throat in order to not open my mouth as I let out, "No…"

Todd rolls over in his bed to face the wall. "Not like you can even see with your injuries."

I shift slightly in my hospital bed, trying to lessen my body aches. The fight with my brother was brutal. Barry popped out my right eye, ripped open my cheek, and broke several of my ribs. He even bit off a chunk of my hand, and they had to amputate my pinky to save the rest of my fingers. The worst injury is my broken knee. Barry kicked it out with, I swear, all of his hate. The damage is as the doctor put it, "Catastrophic." I'll have to have a total knee replacement if I ever hope to walk again.

My military career is over. I was Captain Johnathan Kane, officially a Navy Seal in the peak of my youth at twenty-six. Unofficially the secret ruler Ef earth's go-to man for a top secret mission to protect the world form obliteration. I have saved countless lives with my actions, yet now I am a broken man all because my younger brother went on a killing spree. *God damnit, Barry! What the hell were we thinking? Why did you make me kill you?! Damn fool.*

A nurse comes in with a wheelchair. "Lieutenant Merlin Todd, you have been cleared to go home."

Pointing to myself, I give her a questioning look as if to ask, *What about me?*

She says, "No, unfortunately not." Then she wheels away my roommate, leaving me alone.

The commercial break ends, returning to a daytime drama show. I turn it off because I'd rather listen to my tinnitus than watch that crap. As the silence festers, Barry's final moments play over again in my head. I tried to stop him, tried to knock him out, but he just wouldn't give up. My final plea with him as he lay on the ground, his body broken, while I leaned against the wall with a pistol pointed at him was, "Damn it, Barry. Why did you make me kill you? How the hell am I going to tell Mom?"

From the doorway, a voice quietly speaks, "John?"

This voice should bring me comfort. There stands the most beautiful woman in the world. Long blonde hair tied into a messy bun and her outfit put on in a rush, my wife has been waiting to see me. Her green eyes meet mine. We first met junior year of high school on the track team, and both made it to state in the four-hundred-meter dash. She was a military brat just like me, with younger brothers. I wanted to spend the rest of my life talking with her. Now she is the mother of my soon-to-be child. So why is my first thought after being locked in here for days, fear.

"Vicky." My voice comes out muffled.

Victoria throws her arms over me, ignoring my winces of pain. As she begins to cry on me, I hug her and pat her on the back. Unable to say, "It's alright, everything is alright," I lift one of her arms higher to remove it from around my broken ribs.

She says through tears, "I was so worried about you. They wouldn't tell me what happened and refused to let me see you. They wouldn't even let me leave the hospital."

I want to ask, "Who's they?" But I already know who. Men in black suits who work to keep things secret. Barry's killing spree was on a top-secret government base. They are probably working overtime to keep the truth from slipping out. A security breach on that scale would spawn conspiracies and make the military seem vulnerable.

She holds onto me. "Military Police stood guard at the doors while men in black suits began questioning people."

I pull a few tissues from the wall dispenser for her. She finally lets go, accidentally hitting me right on one of the broken ribs. I wince and let out a grunted curse.

Vicky pulls back finally seeing the full extent of my injuries, "I'm sorry, is that where you were shot?"

I shake my head *no*, then pop my knuckle to say it's broken.

Surprised, Vicky says, "Really? Everyone else from post has some kind of gunshot wound. I even overheard the men in black asking about a gunman. Were you shot in the face?"

I grab her hand with my undamaged fingers in an effort to slow her down, before letting out a guttural, "Sorta," trying my best not to move my lips.

"Oh, sorry. I guess I'm going a bit too fast right now. I was just so worried about you. When they said you had been taken for emergency surgery, I feared the worst."

The doctors tried to save my eyeball after Barry popped it out but ended up just amputating for it had sustained too much damage. I'm honestly surprised Victoria was able to recognize me with my face wrapped up like a mummy.

Victoria sits down next to me, still holding my hand. "So, what are we watching?"

The daytime drama is still playing. I had only hit the

mute button. Did I press the wrong button because of my broken vision or does my hand have additional nerve damage? I give the remote to Victoria, and she changes it to the food network. My stomach grumbles. I won't be able to eat solid food until my cheek heals.

I am kinda glad I can't talk right now. How do I explain to anyone that I murdered my brother? I bet my father already knows. Will he understand? I know Mom won't. How the hell can I ever face her again?

Victoria's beautiful green eyes stay on the television as she talks about the show. She's been getting odd cravings. Last time I was home, she ended up eating an entire jar of pickles and all the peanut butter she could find. Even finding my backup stash of packets I saved from old MREs.

Would she be holding my hand if she knew I beat my brother to death only two days ago? Would she want to raise a child with someone who could kill their own family? Would she still love me, knowing I am a monster?

My grip tightens ever so gently.

CHAPTER 4

JOHN'S NEW LIFE

I WAS CAPTAIN JOHNATHAN KANE, A Special Forces Commando. Now I'm just John as I have been medically discharged from active military service. I should be trying to plan out my life with my wife, but instead I've been fighting with Veterans Affairs.

Arguing with the voice on the other end of the phone, I strain the stitches holding my cheek together to yell, "I've sent you the information five times now! That's all I have! The rest is classified."

The voice is automated, not programmed for complex answers. "I'm sorry. You will have to send it again."

"Can I please talk to a real person?"

"I'm sorry. I do not understand. Please repeat."

"Connect me to a representative."

"I'm sorry. I do not understand. Please repeat."

"Representative!" This sends a jolt of pain through my cheek.

I am answered with a dial tone that switches to a poor recording of a classical song before a different automated voice says, "All representatives are busy. Please stay on the line." Then the four measures of the song are played again before repeating, "All representatives are busy. Please stay on the line."

This will be a while. I turn the phone on speaker, restraining myself from banging my head against the table.

From the next room over, Victoria asks, "Same as yesterday?"

"And the day before that. I don't think there is anyone there to answer the phones. I'm probably going to have to drive down there again. Turn in the paperwork again. Then maybe after the sixth time, I'll be able to schedule an appointment with an orthopedic doctor."

Victoria says, "Or cut out the middleman and hunt down the doctor yourself."

I play the scenario in my head. Staking out the doctor's work and following them home. "I like that plan, but we ain't got bail money if that op goes sideways. Besides…" I flick the aluminum crutches next to me, expecting a clang but getting a dull thud. "My stealth is a bit hampered."

"You could call your father. I'm sure a General could make something happen."

My brother's corpse appears before my eye. "No!" The word comes out louder than I meant. "He hasn't been answering. Probably busy considering the president just won reelection." I hate lying to her, but I am not ready to face my father. I'll probably never be ready.

The VA dick around with me for another week, until my phone wakes me from a blacked-out dream fueled by pain killers and whisky. I reach for my phone in my barely conscious state, and the melted ice packet on my knee splashes to the floor. "Damn it!" After another moment of fumbling through the couch cushions, I find my phone. The caller ID reads Boss.

I answer as professionally as I can manage. "Hello?"

On the other line, Yabechun speaks. His accent has shifted again. "John, are you busy?" Almost sounds british.

The clock on my phone reads three in the morning. "Not particularly."

"Good. Listen, I'm making the rounds right now in China. Had to meet with the big three now that the war has changed. I need you back on post."

"Sir, I've been medically discharged. I ain't no good with a busted leg and one eye."

He yells something in what sounds like Mandarin to someone on his end, then returns to our conversation. "I didn't discharge you. Remember, you work for me at the end of the day. And I still have need of you." He starts yelling in Mandarin again, devolving into an aggressive conversation. It ends with the sound of a hard impact into metal and the breaking of stone. then he returns to our phone call. "Sorry about that. As I was saying, be back on post next Tuesday." He mumbles some calculations. "Scratch that. Two weeks from today. I still need to go to India and meet with the US military committee."

He means all the people in charge of the US military, including my father. "Have you told my father about my situation?"

He answers with a hard, "No."

I don't know if I should be relieved or worried.

Yabechun says, "I'll tell him at the meeting. And don't bother with Veterans Affairs anymore. I have a real solution for your current situation."

Of course, he knows my call history. "Alright, sir." He's not one for questioning.

Two weeks pass by slowly as I waste away the days occupying my time with TV and Victoria goes about her daily routines as if I'm not there. I can't even go grocery shopping since I can no longer drive a manual transmission. The red hotrod my grandfather left me just collects desert dust in the front yard. The vehicle I had given Barry just before his attack. I take a swig of whisky to numb the thoughts of my brother, then adjust myself on the couch, sending a jolt of pain through my knee. I take another swig directly from the bottle.

When the day finally arrives, I have to take Victoria's car as she drives an automatic. On my way out the door, she asks, "When will you be back?"

I hadn't really thought about that. "I don't know. All the things the boss man does is always on a need-to-know basis." I've never said Yabechun's name in her presence. She doesn't need to know what he really is.

She stands between me and the door. "John, I know you well enough that you'll never turn down a fight. But promise me this time you will."

"Vicky, I doubt that's what this is about."

She steps closer to me. "We're starting something beautiful now." She rests her head upon my chest. "I left my life behind for you, and you promised to do the same one day.

No more long trips for either of us. Please promise me that you'll come home."

Before leaving, I gently hold her head and kiss her on the forehead. "I promise to try."

CHAPTER 5

PLANS FOR WAR

That smell is pulling me. The craving for a cigarette is always at the back of my mind. My spine shivers as I make my way to the intoxicating smell, through the open greenery at the center of the Pentagon. The grass looks nice, quite the contrast to my last post in Yuma. It's kind of funny that this uniform was way too hot in the desert and yet it's too cold for the east coast winter.

On a bench under the cloudy sky is the man I'm looking for. In a presidential suit with a long overcoat, his eyes are closed as he takes a long puff of a cigarette.

I say, "Your wife is going to be pissed if she sees you, Mr. President."

Barrack stands for a handshake. "General William Kane, good to see you again." He continues to smoke. "Michael will probably be annoyed, but I just needed something to calm my nerves before dealing with that…" He takes another puff. "*Man*, you've dealt with him longer than I have. How do you handle it?"

"A large cigar and hard liquor after the meetings. But I've

kind of gotten used to it. The risk of the end of the world is just another Tuesday." I catch myself scratching the scar on my cheek again, a permanent reminder of that tiger all those years ago. "I've known that man since Vietnam. He prefers to keep things simple with a phone call or an email these days. However, he's been flying around the world non-stop for the last month. Whatever this is about, it's going to be… how should I put this?"

"Depressing?" the president answers.

I say, "That is one way to look at it. I always like to view it as challenging."

President Obama asks, "Do you trust him?"

I roll up one of my sleeves to show the deep scars along my forearm. "Yes. Because that's what soldiers do in the field. Nothing ever goes to plan, such as a tiger getting to you before the enemy." I roll my sleeve back down. "That man may be an immortal demigod with the devil's eyes, but he is first and foremost a soldier. And I'll trust a soldier over a politician any day."

"I get the picture," the president says with a chuckle in his voice. "And they say my speeches are long."

The alarm on my wristwatch goes off. "It's time, sir."

The president puts out his cigarette in a concrete ashtray attached to a nearby trash bin. "I suppose so."

We make our way through the Pentagon to the most secure location in the world, a series of bunkers four stories underground. These rooms were designed to withstand a nuclear attack and still command the military for a counter offensive. The first door of entry reminds me of a bank vault as its thick steel gears lock shut. Then through a simple wooden door, we enter into a conference room where all the highest-ranking US military officials are already waiting, passing the time with some small talk. Vice President Biden is speaking with Chief of Staff Jack Lew and Secretary of Defense Leon Panetta about their golf game. The directors of the CIA and FBI, whose names I haven't learned yet, are arguing about the jurisdiction of whether a current suspect is a terrorist or a serial killer.

Everyone falls silent as the man with red eyes enters. He stands five-foot-seven, a good deal shorter than the majority of the people in the room. His hairless head reflects the overhead lights. As always, he is dressed in a black suit and tie. "Hello, gentlemen." His voice is loud but not quite a yell. Assistants pass out packets of paper to each person. "Sorry for the delay. I had to make copies for everyone. No slides today."

The soon to be Secretary of State John Kerry says, "I didn't get one."

Everyone looks at the old man with annoyance until the current Secretary of State Clinton says, "Just share with me, John. I don't think he planned on you being here yet."

"Everyone good?" His eyes unblinking, Yabechun looks over us.

He is answered with mumbled agreement by all.

Yabechun continues, "Good. Now, what I am about to share with all of you today will determine the future of not just your country but the entire human race as a whole, for a new kind of war is coming." He takes a moment to look everyone in the eyes, gaging their reactions. His red eyes pierce each of them, yet he skips me for some reason. "Not all of you are fully aware of who I am, and that was by design." He looks at the Chief of Staff and Secretary of State. "You were told that I was the secret chairman of the United Nations, but I am far more than that. Call me Yabechun. I have lived upon this planet for roughly thirteen thousand years. I took the title of Planetary Ruler at the end of the Second World War, with the rise of nuclear weapons."

The few who were unaware now look for confirmation from those in the loop.

"I believe it is best that only the highest officials know of me. There is no need for the average person to bow down to a figure they will never see. This secret has been well guarded for the past sixty-six years. However, this secret has slipped a few times." He looks at Hilary Clinton, the former first lady accusingly.

She says, "In my defense, I did not ask. Bill told me."

Yabechun grumbles, "That man had a hard time with secrets," before continuing, "If you will all turn to the first page of the documents, we shall begin. Last month, a new technology was built in sector two of the Area 51 facility by a young man named Angel Molina."

I flip open the cover page marked as TOP SECRET, finding the first page is titled Angel's Window.

Beginning a slow walk around the conference table, Yabechun continues, "He made a portal that can be separated into two halves. Walking through one portal, you will walk out the other end no matter the space in between them. The sensation of walking through one half is equivalent to walking through a doorway. This can allow for instant travel from one side of the planet to the other or even to the other end of the solar system as long as one end of the portal is placed there. Even allowing for instant communication, provided neither end loses power."

Excitement fills the captive audience and heads turn to each other, sharing surprised and amazed expressions.

Yabechun continues slowly walking around the conference table. "As of now we have two that are fully operational. They are relatively easy to construct as long as the original creator is involved. We have not been able to make one simply using his notes, which would explain why as of now we are the only ones in this galaxy to have this technology."

We continue to the next page.

"All of you should be aware that we currently have spacecrafts of nonterritorial origin. The US has five, Russia has three, and China has two that are all fully operational. The idea was that the most powerful nations on the planet would be able to figure out how these things operate and, if the planet were to be attacked from orbit, the nations on the other side of the globe could launch a counter strike. The unfortunate reality is that would be all we could do. Ten ships are nothing compared to the armadas off-planet empires have built. We are drastically outgunned. Ten interstellar ships each equipped with a nuclear payload is enough to keep possible invaders at bay, but unfortunately, keeping these few ships ready for a possible attack keeps us from expanding out of this solar system, relying on our own ingenuity with rockets. Now, this teleportation technology changes the balance of power in the galaxy. Extraterrestrials will want it, and they take whatever they want. They view us as nothing but…entertainment." He finished with a bit of disgust in his voice.

Air Force General Mark A. Welsh says, "I have a concern regarding an incident in Sector 2 of Area 51 that resulted in several deaths. Was this because of Angel's Window?"

Yabechun looks at me. His demeanor is still calm, his voice remaining dead pan, he says, "One month ago, the creator of the portal escaped the facility but was brought back by Corporal Bartholomew Kane several hours later. Corporal Kane then went on a mass shooting spree killing thirty people, leaving twelve wounded."

Everyone turns their attention to me.

I am unable to hide my surprise, which slowly turns to disappointment. "My son did what?"

"The corporal was stopped twenty minutes later by Captain Johnathon Kane."

I force myself to not turn away, keeping my eyes locked on Yabechun's red goat-like eyes. "Is my son in custody, or did John do what was needed?"

"Captain Johnathon Kane killed Bartholomew Kane in the struggle."

I hold myself steady as my breathing becomes uneasy. I remember the first time I held my son in the hospital. Watching him take his first steps. Hearing his first word, "dada." Teaching him the essentials of survival, and breaking up squabbles between my sons. I can clearly remember the last time I spoke with Barry before his last deployment. I start to bite down, holding back my emotions.

Everyone is quiet as a sixty-year-old man battles his emotions until President Obama asks, "Do you need to step out?"

I force everything down, making sure my eyes are dry.. "No. No! Please…continue."

Yabechun keeps his gaze fixed on me. "We do not know why Corporal Bartholomew Kane went on his rampage.

However, we believe it was a personal reason, not connected to the teleporter."

Hillary Clinton asks before Yabechun can continue. "Why don't we just share this new technology with the aliens? Couldn't this lead to better relations with them?"

Yabechun finally releases me of his horrid gaze and continues his slow pace around the conference table. "No, that would be equivalent to giving the Germans Atomic bombs in the middle of World War Two in hopes of peace. This technology will allow us to expand beyond Earth. We can become a multiplanetary species. Humanity will finally have a unifying goal. There will no longer be a need to hide behind different nations as we reach beyond our dying star." He reaches up to grab this invisible goal, then closes his fist and pulls it back down. "There will be new enemies."

Everyone turns to the next page of the packet.

"The original plan was to have the largest three nations fight each other to clear the table of undesirable populations and force innovation. Now that we have a different enemy at our doorstep, we will need every person on the same side. I have spent the last month gathering information on every major military force, speaking with government leaders, front line troops, and my many spies. I wasn't concerned when everyone was going to be fighting one another. After all, I hold control over almost all nuclear weapons, preventing you people from ending all life on this planet. Now I have seen firsthand how well the military budgets were spent.

"In regard to Russia's stockpiles, I am greatly disappointed. They were meant to directly compete with this nation, but the corruption has grown too deep. President

Putin put his friends in charge of everything, with zero oversight, resulting in the majority of their military budget going to aristocrat's fancy yachts, lavish mansions, and living decadent lives. Worst of all, most of their weapon stockpiles from the Cold War have vanished. I have sent some of my people to investigate where everything has gone, but most likely they were sold off to smaller nations. The former Soviet Union will be forced to use leftover weapons from the second World War." Frustration in his voice rises, "And a bunch of nukes are unaccounted for. Some were just painted trees in missile silos!" He pauses in his encircling walk. "I hope for everyone's sake those were always trees and not sold to unauthorized individuals."

We turn to the next page, labeled China.

Yabechun resumes his slow walk, his hands behind his back now. "China has spent a decent amount on weaponry, creating a strong military presence on that side of the planet, as well as a strong sense of nationalism. The Chinese people view all outside nations as threats, especially the US. However, they lack people, food, and clean water."

I need to say something in this meeting, prove I'm not broken with grief. Clearing my throat, I say, "Don't they have a massive population? They're a major problem in the pacific."

Yabechun stops his walk right behind me. "They do have a large population but not of fighting age. The one child policy failed to merely slow the population, instead causing the next generation to be less than a third the size of the last. None of them wanted girls, causing many unfortunate souls to be abandoned or killed, leading to a population without mates. Mixed with poor food supplies and low water quality, this has created a shrinking population that must now care for the larger generation of senior citizens. Direct confrontation would cripple their population into collapse."

He resumes his slow pace around the table. "Although right next to China, India has had a massive boom in population. Their military is about the same as China technologically. They will prove to be very useful in the upcoming war."

The table turns to the last page of assets, titled USA.

"Now we get to all of you. I wanted this to be my last meeting because I knew the majority of the war would fall upon this nation. You people spend more money on your military than all the other countries combined. This nations' entire economy is practically sustained by the war machine. It is one of the few things that brings a real smile to my face. So, I will say thank you for not dropping the ball, unlike your competitors. Combined with your years of experience fighting wars across the seas, you know better than most the logistics of fighting a war on foreign soil."

Yabechun stops to pat the president on the shoulder. "Keep up the good work."

The final portion of the packet is labeled, The Enemy, with a picture of a gray humanoid creature with black, lifeless eyes pointed forward, small slits for a nose, and small nubs where ears should be.

"Our enemy is called the Anunnaki, and they have been an interstellar species for at least fifty thousand years."

The packet is full of pictures of the gray creatures on operating tables, displaying their confusing organ structures. Each one looks oddly thin. *Is it their natural state to look so malnourished?*

"Their leadership has remained stagnant for those fifty

thousand years. An average citizen's lifespan was expanded to range from five hundred years to a thousand Earth years through horrid experiments thousands of years ago. Their height fluctuates from four-foot-one to ten-foot, depending on where they are from in the galaxy. The smaller ones tend to be stronger as they are from planets with a greater gravity than our own. One of their worlds has roughly triple our own gravitational pull. All information about them has been obtained by capturing Anunnaki, as performing espionage on a species that reads minds and lives light years away is rather difficult at this time."

Barack asks, "How can you trust any information gathered this way?"

He smiles, showing his perfect white teeth. "We have perfected being…persuasive."

I immediately understand his implications. "How has torturing these creatures not led to retaliation?"

Yabechun continues, "Does the US go to war when an American citizen commits a crime in a foreign nation?"

"No, that would be ridiculous."

"Exactly!" His pace around the table remains the same controlled walk even with excitement in his voice. "As I said, the enemy views humans as nothing but entertainment. They have two sexes, the same as us males and females; however, they do not reproduce with one another very often. With such abnormally long lives and the ability to genetically clone new bodies, sex lost its purpose to build families unlike most human societies. Leading down a twisted path of sexual exploration, then with the rediscovery of our species, they started taking our people for nefarious, perverted purposes. That is why most survivors claim to have been anally probed. As such, we are within our right to protect our people.

"However, this tends to result in the destruction of the spacecraft. Our advancements in anti-aircraft munitions have that effect. That's if we are in the right place at the right time to deploy countermeasures into their flight path. We have been able to scavenge some of their unique technology, but we can't reproduce or repair to the same quality as the elements do not occur naturally on Earth and when we try to recreate them artificially, they are unstable, decaying quickly.

"The Anunnaki survivors are imprisoned in one of two facilities, depending on where they were shot down. Either the Arctic or deep underground in sector three of the Area 51 facility."

Barack asks, "How much have you learned?"

"We have learned about them biologically. Every one of them possesses an enlarged frontal lobe on their brain, allowing them to perceive a high state of unconsciousness naturally. We exist in the third dimension and can vaguely see the fourth dimension as the flow of time. They can easily see into the fifth dimension and bend it, giving them a form of Telekinesis. They also discovered how to extend their lives into near immortality through horrible experimentation. Most of their elder ruling class has kept that power to themselves. The rest of their population have only been gifted hyper extended lifespans. We have learned how to kill them. Most die as easily as any other organic being. We've even created some biological agents that can affect them. The elder will require a more direct approach, decapitation is the only true guarantee. I discovered that personally in my lifetime."

The next page is labeled Enemy Weaponry.

"Our enemy has not advanced much in the way of military power in the past thirteen thousand years, for they have grown complacent. Living in a utopian society without any conflict on their home worlds for generations, aside from their five living leaders, none of their population has endured any kind of hardship. Living without sickness or crime, only stealing sentient lifeforms to satisfy their urges. However, that does not mean we can take this threat lightly.

"With their telekinesis they can move any object fifty feet from their form, allowing them to push a meteorite at an intended target from the safety of a spaceship. A large enough rock can completely decimate a planet. A well-placed strike into glaciers will cause massive flooding on a global scale, reducing the planetary population to a mere fraction of what stood before." He stops his walk, his face more stoic than normal. "That's how it ended last time."

He continues his pace. "But we clawed our way back from the brink, fighting tooth and nail to become the most terrifying sentient species in the galaxy. We have developed technology that they never even considered on the battle-field, for it is far too cruel. Chemical weapons, biological agents, and psychological warfare. Humans are the only species that will poison itself just to spite itself."

Yabechun pulls out a foot-long silver cylinder from his black coat. "Now, we will have to worry about their warriors in addition to their extensive armada of interstellar crafts. A subspecies of theirs, each standing at six feet tall, from a planet with twice our gravitational pull. They live in a feudal society with the sole purpose of perfecting fighting skills. They were not given extended lives by their leaders in their home world. They developed a powerful weapon during a failed rebellion against the ruling home world. The warriors failed their Queue but kept this."

He presses a button on the side of the cylinder, extending a long red blade that lets out a slight hum. "Each Anunnaki warrior uses four of these blades. The hilt is steel with carbon nanotubes for strength, while the blade is a super conductor containing highly concentrated plasma vibrating at high frequency to keep it hot and contained." He gently swings the blade around to demonstrate his sword skills before slicing the concrete floor like butter.

"We have captured very few warriors due to their ability to block automatic fire with their telekinetic abilities. There are always a few flying around our solar system, waiting for a chance to rescue their imprisoned kin. We keep them distracted by projecting out our entertainment to the cosmos. Hollywood is our species' most useful tool to stay relevant in the galaxy, aside from one other fact." He rolls up his sleeve before using the glowing red blade to cut his wrist ever so gently. He shows his captive audience the open wound as his blood quickly pulls his flesh back together, sealing the wound with a light scar. "They know to rightfully fear me!" He retracts the blade into its cylinder before placing it back in his pocket. "Unfortunately, we have not been able to replicate this technology. More elements we can't stably recreate. But all elements they have on their home world are ripe for the taking."

He stops his walk directly behind the president again. "I believe in all of you to win what is to come. We have at least another year until the portal technology can be fully implemented, but until then, every nation's military will be on high alert for an imminent threat. The people can continue to believe the war will be between yourselves. Then when an external threat attacks what we hold sacred, we will unite as one to repeal the enemy." He collects all the information on the teleporter. "Any questions, call me, but under no circumstances do you speak of the teleporter in the open or else we will be dealing with a massive threat before we are truly ready. Study the rest of the information on the alien threat. We will reconvene in one month to discuss further plans of attack."

Assistants collect everyone's papers except for me. Yabechun takes the time to take mine. He says no words only nods at me. An unspoken show of respect for containing my emotions. Then he leaves while his assistants incinerate the top secret technology.

Keeping my emotions on lockdown, I shake hands with everyone as we all mingle from one small group to the next, discussing what an extraterrestrial war could look like. We are given flash drives containing all the information gathered about our future enemy before leaving. I need to research what we're up against before I can make a real strategy. The current chief of staff for the Air Force, Mark A. Welsh, jokes, "The Marines don't strategize. Just give those crayon eaters a direction to shoot. In this case, it will be up."

I give a sarcastic chuckle. "Well, someone is going to have to hit everything the *Chair Force* misses." Then I turn to leave. I have a more pressing matter than trading jokes with the other military branches.

I get in my government issued black SUV. Unlike my colleagues of similar rank, I prefer to drive myself, maintaining my independence. Pulling into an empty parking lot, I finally let out all my emotions, slamming my hands on the steering wheel, my eyes beginning to water. I can't believe I'm crying real tears for the first time in my adult life. I let out a cry of anger mixed with pain of suffering only a parent who has lost a child knows.

Then I sit there quietly trying to remember my son as he was. The punk with his mother's hair. Why would he do such a thing? Where did I fail as a father? Maybe I shouldn't have forced him to witness his aunt's execution. I thought it was important for him to see such things before joining the military.

"How the hell am I going to tell Susan?" I plead with my head against the steering wheel now.

We accepted that possibility of loss. That's the risk of this path in life, but Barry killed our own people, forcing his brother to stop him. I am proud that John rose to the occasion. I don't think I could have made the same call. I'll tell my wife that Barry died overseas heroically. She does not need to hate her oldest son for killing her middle child.

CHAPTER 6

LIVE AGAIN

TIME IS A NEVER-ENDING SPIRAL trying to reach an impossible conclusion, with brief moments of recognition but always just out of reach. It's shaped just beyond, in the darkness, yet so close I could touch it. I need to reach it. Forward, always forward. I want it to end. I need it to end. Yet it continues on and on forever.

I am Jason.

My eyes open to a bright light, blinking slowly as my world begins to focus. A white room with a sink, cabinets, and a desktop computer. There is a camera pointed at me from above the only door. I slowly sit up in what appears to be a hospital bed. An IV with multiple tubes is dripping clear in one arm while a white liquid is fed into the other, the bags are almost empty. With an adjustment of my legs, I feel a catheter attached below.

Am I still in custody? Why do I feel ill? My body aches more than normal. Wait a second, my left eyelid isn't drooping anymore.

I move my left hand to test its dexterity. Everything moves fine but with a lack of muscle.

The entire left side of my body was paralyzed after my stroke. I haven't had full control of that hand in years, despite my best efforts. "Oh my god. I am hungry." I haven't had an appetite since the state put me on medication for my brain tumor. My vision is still blurry. I feel like I'm seeing double. Then the IV machine starts to beep an alarm. "Oh, shit! Shut up. What did I do?"

A man in a long white coat and green scrubs walks in with a clipboard. I see him moving as if there were two of him, each image delayed behind the last. He looks to be in his late fifties with a comb-over. He adjusts his bifocals as he examines the charts. Before pressing a button on the IV pump to stop the alarm, he says, "Good to see you awake, Mister Baker." His voice is calm, with a possible Midwestern accent.

I don't say anything, sizing up this doctor while trying to focus my vision. What are his intentions?

"Not much for talking. That's fine. Well, let's take a look real quick." The first image turns on a flashlight, then the second image repeats the process as the light momentarily blinds me.

"Normal pupil dilatation. That's good." Then he puts his stethoscope on.

As the second image copies, I feel the cold metal touch my back and almost flinch.

"Relax and take deep breaths."

I do as asked, reaching into his pocket while he's close. Gently, I steal what feels to be a pen.

The doctor steps back. "You seem relatively healthy. All things considered." He sits on a nearby stool with wheels.

I say, "Healthy but dying," as I hide the pen under my leg.

"Well, Jason. Can I call you Jason?"

He doesn't give me a chance to answer.

"Well, that's the thing." He looks down, flipping through the papers on his clipboard.

It looks like he's flipping each page three times. What is wrong with my eyes?

"I don't believe you have a brain tumor. Or if you did, there is nothing remaining."

My eyes narrow. Now the doctor is finally standing still, causing the multiple images to shrink into him. "What do you mean? Doctor no name."

"Well, judging by your medical records, you have absolutely no family history of cancerous tumors, which would make the appearance of one an anomaly but not unheard of. What really troubles me is that your diagnosis came from only one MRI scan, done the year before. There is no record if you were rescanned, and I can't find any record of blood work. And looking at this recent MRI."

He rolls on the stool to the nearby computer and pulls up two MRI scans. "Comparing this one from last week to the one from a few years ago."

The older one looks really fuzzy, even with my straining vision.

"I've looked at hundreds of brain scans in my time as a doctor. Even in the first years of MRI scans, I've never seen one this blurry. They should have rescanned you. That being said, your Hippocampus does look a bit inflamed, but that could be the picture's resolution."

He points to the clear MRI scan. "As you can see clearly in this scan last week, there are no growths in your brain. Your Hippocampus does appear to be a tad larger than normal. That, with the added stress of being in confinement and the many fights you were apparently involved in, is what likely led to your stroke." He returns to the chart. "Now, looking at the medications you were on, in addition to an incorrect dosage of chemotherapy, you were also given an absolute criminal amount of Oxycontin, especially for a minor. I would say this was malpractice, or more likely given your history, the prison doctors were trying to get rid of you. It is a miracle you survived. Tell me, did you fight to not take your meds?"

I keep my eye on the door. "So, I got a round of chemo and been taking pills and pain meds for no fucking reason?" That doesn't make sense. I'm supposed to die. This timeline doesn't need me anymore. I need to get out of here. "Wait… did you say last week? How long have I been here?"

"I'm sorry, that's not for me to say."

"Then who is?" I prepare to rip these tubes out of my arm.

"I can't say. I am truly sorry. You should be thankful they didn't try to operate on you. An unnecessary surgery on that scale could have killed you or left you in a vegetative state. The chemo did stop you from entering puberty properly. Lucky for you, we are on the cutting edge of medical science here, using technology that very few have access to. While you were in your coma, we injected you with fresh stem cells to bring feeling back into your left side. It should also allow you to go through puberty properly, being that you are still near the age you would go through it naturally. One nice thing about being young, you still bounce when you fall."

Holding the pen tight under my leg, I ask, "What coma?"

The doctor pauses, realizing that he said too much, before accepting that there's no turning back now. "As it pertains to your health, I can say you were put into a drug induced coma for an extended period of time to treat you properly. According to your record, you have quite a history of violence."

Through gritted teeth, I force out, "How long?" I lean more forward, preparing to lunge.

"Again, I can't say." The doctor knocks on the door without leaving his seat.

In walks a nurse with a medical mask and her hair covered, as well as a large man in a camouflage uniform.

I quickly hide the pen back under my leg while the nurse unhooks the tubes from my arms.

I need to replan this. That's a US army uniform. So, I'm in military custody. I'm not getting away from them in my current condition, but I need answers. What does the military want with me? I'm an unhinged delinquent. Then the pieces click. *Angel…what did you do? I was meant to die! Did you tell them about me?*

When the nurse turns her back after finishing unhooking the IV tubes, I lunge to grab her hair, pulling her off balance. Holding the pen to her temple, I demand, "Where is—?!"

A large fist impacts me hard in the nose, dropping me back onto the bed. The guard takes the pen before handcuffing my arm to the bed. My vision blurs with dark shadows as the flow of time becomes visible once again. With the taste of blood in my mouth, I try to say, "What have you people done with Angel?"

The doctor stands up. "Damn savage. Nurse, please get some gauze for the poor kid." He reaches down and pulls my nose back into place with a quick pop.

The guard says, "My orders are to keep the prisoner under control by any means, Doc."

"He's a patient, not a prisoner."

The material world falls away again.

CHAPTER 7

FIRST STEPS

THE INFINITE SPIRAL ENCIRCLES US all. Time will never care as it forever moves. Will I be lost here? No! I have to remember who I am.

Jason, I am Jason Baker. My friend needs me. I have to save Angel!

My eyes open on the same small medical examination room. My face hurts, but at least my nose is straight. There is a small cup of applesauce beside me. Beyond hungry, I strain to eat it with my weak left arm. There is still a lingering haze at the edge of my sight. No matter how many times I blink, the haze remains. It feels different from a concussion. When I hold my arm still, the images faze into one. Then when I move the spoonful of food, I bite down onto a vision that is not there, followed by hitting my mouth with the intended sustenance. I think I'm seeing slightly into the future.

Must be another side effect of my mind coming back in time. Every time I made a significace change I would get a vision of the new future that always concluded with the nuclear explosion, my stroke happened when I changed the future away from the war. Now that I have lost my connection to my original timeline, this is likely the effect. I think I can use this to my advantage, but it will require some getting used to.

As I make a mess of myself, I realize I am not alone. The guard that punched me stands at the only door, his eyes focused forward. I awkwardly finish my meal before breaking the silence, "You got a name, big man?"

The guard stands unflinching.

"I'm Jason, kidnapped prisoner," I say, trying to lighten the mood.

No acknowledgement.

"You know, we could try to have a conversation. I've been starved of communication."

The guard just stands there, a near perfect statue.

"Not even a name? Fine, I'll call you Stone, because you're a stone statue."

He still just stands there.

"Say something, *anything*, even a cough or a sneeze. Are you a robot?"

He takes a hard inhale through his nose.

"I hate you."

We return to silence.

How the hell do I get out of here, and more importantly, how do I find Angel? I'm not in a prison anymore. This looks like a military facility, and there are no bars. My body is too weak to fight my way out. I don't even know if I can walk after being stuck in bed for so long. I've apparently been in a coma for a month, and I was strapped to a bed in juvey before that. I don't know if my legs will even work. That doctor seems to have good intentions, so I might be able to use that to my advantage. I think my best bet will be to bide my time, let my body heal. Maybe they'll take me right to Angel.

The silence is broken by a knock at the door, then the doctor enters, wearing the same green scrubs and white coat but without any pens in his pockets this time.

He says, "I'm glad to see you finished eating. Now we are going to test your strength." He turns to the unmoving guard. "Would you please uncuff the patient."

The guard says, "My orders are to secure the prisoner."

The doctor says, "And we are quite secure here. Nowhere for him to run too." He looks back at me. "It's been a few hours, plenty of time for the boy to have calmed down."

I raise my untethered hand in surrender. "I'll be nice."

The guard unlocks the cuff on my wrist, whispering into my ear, "If you try anything again, I will drop you. Understand?"

I feel the massive gap between our strengths. "Yes, sir."

After so long of being stuck in a bed, I struggle to get to the mattress edge. The doctor offers out his hands to assist me. I ignore the offer. This has to be on my own. My body shakes from the strain as I straighten up. My right foot lands, but when I move my left leg, the stiffness doesn't let me move properly, causing me to stumble forward.

The doctor catches me. "I've got you. Take it easy."

My grip tightens around the doctor's arms as I force myself forward, determined to make it to the door. If I could just reach the door, I could gain more of an understanding about this new prison. The guard moves to directly block me as the doctor veers our walk in a small circle around the room, right back to the bed.

"There you go, very good."

My body trembles from the strain, but I make another attempt to walk.

The doctor reaches to help me.

"No! I need this." My steps are small as I walk in a straight line to the adjacent wall and then back, seeing each step before I make it.

Just focus. Remember your training. Never give up.

In a few more steps, I reach my bed again and rest upon it. My body trembling, I say, "Alright, Doc, now what?"

The doctor types something into his notes on the computer. When he finishes, he says, "This is going to take some time, but I believe we can rehabilitate you."

CHAPTER 8

COLD WORDS

I STILL HAVE MY MILITARY IDENTIFICATION badge. Captain Johnathan Kane, authorization Top Secret. They didn't punch a hole in it when I was discharged, but according to my boss, I wasn't officially discharged. Yet I have filled out paperwork that says otherwise. I love the structure of military life, but I swear no one really knows what they're doing around here. Just a bunch of eighteen-year-olds playing soldier while bureaucrats plan things out from afar.

Now I find myself in Yabechun's grand office of sector 2, what the outside world refers to as Area 51, waiting in a plastic chair. It's the kind they had in public school. Cheap plastic does not give proper back support for a full-grown man. After a few minutes, my back starts to ache. I look out the window to see if any planes are landing. Looks all clear, so I decide I might as well use this very rare opportunity.

With my crutches, I slowly make my way around the office, passing the many file cabinets, taking my time to look at every single picture Yabechun has. There's one of him shaking hands with President Truman and another with

Joseph Stalin. He's not smiling in either picture. It looks like his bald head caught the flash in these pictures. I wonder if he waxes it to keep it shiny. There is a picture of him giving a speech at what looks like the United Nations. It's in black and white, must have been when he first established the UN. The last picture on this side of the room is of a completely destroyed city. Absolutely nothing remains standing except for a two-story building with a bent frame and a partial skeleton of a metal dome. This is Hiroshima right after the first Atomic Bomb dropped. This picture is paired with what looks like an even older picture of the same city from when cameras were first made. He must never want to forget what nuclear weapons can do.

I hobble over to the other side of the room. All these pictures are of Yabechun's military outfits. In one of his Airborne division in World War II, his face looks horrifically scarred. I only know it's him because no one else could suffer wounds like that and survive. In the picture of him in a dark Civil War-era uniform, he looks far less scarred. It's strange that he has a Katana at his side. I pause to pick up the framed photograph of Yabechun with my great grandfather. Great-Grandpa Jack in his French Foreign Legion uniform with that unmistakable apostrophe X on his left cheek, grinning with Yabechun, who looks like a burn victim fresh out of Hell. My great-grandfather always had a smile on his face, all the way up to his hundredth birthday. I know that man went through more crazy shit than I will ever know, but I only ever remember him having a smile. Even when he would tell the messed-up stories of his life with a humorous twist.

An unmistakable voice says, "I miss that man every day.

I wish he was still around. Sure could use his wit in these trying times."

Still holding the picture in my hand, I spin around on my good leg to stand at attention. "Yabechun, sir."

He makes his way to his desk and logs into his computer. "At ease. Please, I had the chair brought in just for you."

I am not sitting in that plastic piece of junk again. "With all due respect, sir, I would rather stand."

"Suit yourself. Give me a second to send out an email." He starts typing incredibly fast. "I appreciate how quick global communication is nowadays, but I would be lying if I didn't say I missed the simplicity of the old days."

"Which old days do you refer to, sir?" I ask as I place the framed photo back in its place.

He finishes typing. "Either the 1880s or the 1920s. I could send a letter to anywhere in the world, or if I really needed, I could send a telegraph. Not that I had any real emergency's back then." Relaxing in his simple desk chair, he locks his red goatlike eyes on me. "Now, John, there are some important matters I want to discuss with you."

I hobble back in front of his desk. "What type of matters, sir? Do you need a new secretary? Your current one was watching cartoons on his computer when I got here."

He shakes his head. "No, you are overqualified for that job." His eyes never blink. "I need someone to be all the places I can't. Someone I can trust beyond a shadow of a doubt. Someone that can make the tough calls. End one life to save many, even if that life was family."

I feel a pit in my stomach. Barry's final moments before pulling the trigger flashes across my mind.

"You have proven your loyalty to the mission beyond anything your father could bear."

I push the image of Barry's corpse away. Remembering my promise to Vicky, I let out a quiet, "No."

Yabechun sits up straight in his chair. "I'm sorry, what was that?"

"No." My voice is as weak as before. "I made a promise to my wife that I would come home to her."

He stands up. "You clearly don't understand what is at stake." But rather than attack me, he turns to look out the window, to the airfield, his voice sorrowful. "How could you know? I am the only one that remembers the old world." He turns back to me. "This world is about to fight a war with an enemy that sees us as mere insects. The last time they came here, they wiped out more than two thirds of all life on this planet. With the push of a rock from space, they flooded this planet, drowning my people and destroying almost everything. Now they are about to come again. I will have to lead our planet's people in this war from the front lines. I will need great men to fight alongside me." He walks toward me. "This war will encompass the entire globe."

He stands just before me, looks me dead in the eyes. "Now I give you the chance to save it and you refuse, to protect your wife's feelings." With a singular finger, he pushes me.

My balance is terrible with my bad leg, so I fall straight onto my ass.

Yabechun stands above me. "What kind of protection can you provide now?"

Feeling like a helpless child, I don't answer.

"I offer you a chance to not only save Victoria and your

unborn child but the strength to save every person on earth."
He extends his hand down to me.

He's right. What good am I to my family in my current
state? I am a soldier, unable to fight. He hasn't said how he
will get me back into fighting condition, but I don't doubt
the resources at his disposal. I accept his hand.

He lifts me with ease, saying, "Now come with me."

Yabechun leads me out of his office. He is at least a foot
shorter, yet walks so much faster. I struggle to keep up on
my crutches. We go to an elevator at the end of a short hallway. He swipes an ID badge he has in his pocket and types
in 1945, opening the doors. Then we enter and he presses
B1 on the button panel.

"Now that you will be taking a stance at my side. Your
body will need to be fixed. One missing finger is fine, but
something needs to be done about your sight and knee.
Thankfully, steps in both genetics and robotics have come a
long way. Far beyond what the public is aware of."

This all feels a bit fast. "I should tell my wife about this.
You know, in case anything goes haywire."

"Don't be a coward. You will be fine. You'll be part of the
seventh generation of this program. All the bugs have been
mostly worked out."

Wait... He's leaving out some key information. "Seventh
generation?"

He's facing away from me, but I can see a smirk on the
edge of his face. "The enhanced soldier program started
during World War II, one by the Axis Powers and one by
the Allied Forces. The only field ready product from that
war was meth-fueled Nazis soldiers. After the war, I collected
as many of the Nazi scientists as I could with operation

Paperclip. I'm sure you were aware of that program—that's how the US got the rocket scientists. Although, that is what brought back the attention of the extraterrestrials to begin with."

I did know about the Nazi scientists, but I keep my mouth shut during this long elevator ride.

"The next two generations failed, but progress was made. We cracked the human genome many years before the public did. We have had access to stolen advanced alien technology after all. Above all, our scientists have had access to a very unique subject." He turns around as the elevator doors open. "Me."

We step forth from the elevator to more offices with tinted windows. "With direct access to my unique genetic code and the knowledge of how I came to be, we have been able to partially recreate my strength in other people. Of course, not to my current level. You will not live forever, but you will be enhanced to a level of strength, durability, and endurance far beyond any of the average soldier. One side effect your eyes will look like mine. They tend to weird people out but I can see more colors on the electromagnetic spectrum."

His phone buzzes and he answers, annoyed at first. "What is it?" Quickly cheering up, he says, "Oh, really now, that changes things. I'll be right there." He turns back to me. "Quick detour, John."

Yabechun turns around, walking right past me. He didn't say wait here so I follow. We turn down several other hallways. This place is like a maze. Then we stop outside a door labeled Recovery Room 2. With a knock at the door, a man in a white medical coat and green scrubs comes out. I would guess he's in his fifties with that bad combover.

Yabechun says, "Good morning, Doctor Matsushino. I was informed that the patient has awakened."

Matsushino says, "Yes, sir. He was a bit rambunctious earlier, but Stevenson corrected that. The boy was able to walk around the room with little to no help. I believe his recovery will proceed well."

"Good. Oh, by the way, this is Johnathan Kane. He's entering into the enhanced soldier program."

The doctor shakes my good hand. "Pleasure to meet you. I'll be seeing you around here then."

Yabechun opens the door, gesturing to a guard to leave. The guard is a young man in a military uniform with a tactical belt similar to what policemen have. When he passes me, he gives me a disgusted look before walking away. *What a punk.*

Matsushino says, "Give me a call if you need anything. I'll be in my office." The he walks in the opposite direction of the guard.

Yabechun says, "Come along, John. This is important."

But before entering, he puts on his sunglasses and whispers to me, "Keep quiet though."

The room is small but not unreasonable. Just like any medical observation room I've been in for a doctor's visit. Alone on the edge of a hospital bed is a thin, pale teenager. The boy needs to eat a real meal and get some sunlight. His hair is just starting to grow from a previously bald head. What seems off is just how tense this kid is. He doesn't have a lot of muscle, but he holds himself in a way that he could strike at any moment. Who is this kid? Some new recruit for the enhancement program? He's about the age to enlist.

Yabechun speaks gently, "Hello, Jason. How are you today?"

Still on edge, Jason asks, "Do I know you?"

Yabechun says, "No, you shouldn't, but I know an awful lot about you." He takes a step closer to the boy. "Jason C. Baker. Age 18. Born to Ronald S. Baker and Maryann C. Baker in Yuma, Arizona. The youngest of three siblings, Peter S. Baker and Anna C. Baker. A boy with average grades who one day committed aggravated assault against five class-mates, then received several more aggravated assault charges in Juvenile Hall."

Jason does not act impressed. "So what? You read my file. I swear I know you from somewhere."

Yabechun continues, "You were misdiagnosed with a terminal brain tumor. Now—"

"Now you shady government people have me. Get to the point Q-ball."

Keeping his composure, Yabechun says, "The point is, how did a kid with average grades in math figure out the equations for portal technology when smarter beings have dedicated their entire lives to similar pursuits and never gotten anything close to what you have."

Trying to look tougher than he is, Jason straightens up before asking, "Where is Angel?"

Yabechun says, "Safe."

"How safe?"

"Safe enough to keep working."

"Then what do you need me for? I gave Angel everything I had."

"I need to know how you came up with it. Until then, you are a security risk. Now you can tell me, or"—Yabechun removes his sunglasses revealing his red goat like eye—"I can extract the answer from you."

Jason mumbles, "So that's why you wear sunglasses inside." He sits back down on his hospital bed. "What is the likelihood of me living? The truth is unbelievable."

Yabechun says, "I have seen the unbelievable many times in my long life."

There is a slight smirk on Jason's face. He knows more than he should. "You didn't answer my question. Not like it's the first time I've faced death." His eyes lock with Yabechun's. "I'm from the future. One where a world war ripped across the globe. I was sent back in the light of a nuclear explosion. I am the collective memories of many Jasons from every change I made in this timeline. I know the formulas because I've traveled through the fabric of time many times. My connection to that future was severed when I gave Angel my notebook. I don't know how he applied my formulas or what he built, but it prevented the war. Now here we are."

The two maintain an unblinking eye contact for a full minute before Yabechun asks, "How did that war start?"

Without breaking eye contact, Jason says, "December 2012, North Korea fired a nuclear missile at Hawaii and a second one at Russia, but I only ever heard rumors about where the second one hit."

Yabechun exchanges a quick look with me.

How does this kid know about my mission? The only other people that knew the missiles' paths are all dead by my hand. Who is this kid?

Smiling with his perfect white teeth, Yabechun finally

says, "Interesting. It seems everything is in order here." He turns to leave.

"What about me?" Jason asks, showing concern for the first time.

Yabechun says, "You will be kept here to assist your fellow delinquent on his top-secret project. We will be entering into mass production soon. I don't like to waste assets."

We leave the boy alone in his room and continue deeper into this underground facility. I ask, "Was it wise to just leave that kid unguarded?"

Yabechun says, "I am not worried. He has no means of opening that door. Besides, he has no reason to want to leave. Not until he sees his friend."

We reach a door labeled Enhancement Department. "More importantly, I now know we are on the correct path. Based upon what that boy said, the original world war plan would have failed. Human conflict now can only devolve into a nuclear holocaust." He rubs his hands together excitedly. "Now the goal is to focus that hatred off this world."

CHAPTER 9

REBUILT

BLACKNESS. *WHY IS IT DARK? How long has it been dark?*

"Remember your mission, John." The words echo, calling me back to the light.

My new eyes open to bright fluorescent lights. I can't feel a single thing. I know I have a body, but everything is numb. They must have put me on some really good drugs.

I remember Yabechun's words before I went under. "The easy part will be the beginning. You will receive a number of injections to alter your genetic code. The bone marrow injections are going to hurt, but they will pale in comparison to what comes after. Your body will be torn apart, and with your altered genetic code, it will build back stronger than before."

Before I could protest, he said, "You will be given anesthetic and pain meds to ease the discomfort. I was not given such luxuries, as my body was broken before being discarded into the ocean without skin." He then picked up a steel paper weight and crushed it with one hand. "You will only receive a fraction of my strength. Do not squander this power."

My skin feels tight as I begin to move. Sitting up in bed to feel my new body, I don't feel stronger, only constricted, as if my muscles have exercised to exhaustion.

Nurses remove my bandage as all manner of tests are conducted. Blood taken, head scanned, and waste analyzed, all to ensure my body accepted the treatment. When I take my first steps, a deep, unrivaled pain shoots from the bottom of my foot all throughout my body. Every nerve ending is signaling that my skin is on fire, dropping me to one knee, where even more pain rushes through me. I bite down hard to hold back my scream, letting out only a guttural grown of agony.

One of the nurses runs off to get me pain meds as I am consumed by a burning bane.

Yabechun stops her. "No, he needs to accept this part."

I yell out, "What have you done to me?"

"You have been reborn in my image."

My eyes water as I can no longer hold back how much everything hurts. "You promised me meds!"

He stands above me, his red eyes showing no signs of empathy. "Only for the surgery. Now your body is remembering the trauma." He kneels down close to me. "I told you this would be hard. Now prove to me you are worthy of my power."

Every ounce of my body burns—death would be better. I have to channel it. *Remember your SEAL training*. In that moment, my primal instinct to survive kicks in. As my pain turns into hatred, my hand shoots out and wraps around Ya-bechun's throat. One hand is all I need to completely wrap around his neck. He doesn't react, only fueling my hatred. I squeeze with all of my new strength.

Yabechun smiles as he continues to easily breath. "That's the spirit." He casually peels my fingers away. "Now pick yourself up. Your training has begun."

I am not given back my clothes after this excruciating experience but PT gear instead. I am put through grueling physical training similar to what I experienced to become a Navy SEAL. Only the weights are doubled. All the while this deep pain burns through my entire body.

Yabechun's training includes more than just strength training. "You need to stay flexible, or else you will be trapped by your own muscles." So, he keeps me on an aerobics training path too, working all my muscle groups.

The feeling of growing strength eclipse the trauma my body was forced through, but in the quiet moments in between exercises, that deep burning pain bubbles back to the service. A shot of medication can calm it for a time but never long enough.

Days bleed together as time loses all meaning. The only thing in my mind is my family's moto, "To be born a Kane is to be born a killer."

My endurance has increased such that I can run for days with over a hundred pounds of weight on my back. My max speed exceeds the current Olympic world record. I can run a full marathon in an hour and thirty minutes. Before, my best time was only thirteen miles in about an hour fifty. I have gone down from seven-minute miles to under four-minute miles. More importantly, I don't feel any hindrance in my knee. My raw strength has improved to an unbelievable level. From the ground, I can launch myself to my feet with one hand while wearing an extra hundred pounds on my back.

I am becoming the perfect killer.

When I finally get a chance to see myself in a mirror, I see that all signs of age have been pulled away. Every part of me has doubled, my body transformed into a muscular monstrosity. I'm forced to bend down to use the sink now that I've grown much taller. My eyes are no longer green with hints of blue like my father's. Now they are blood red, the same as Yabechun. The missing eyeball was replaced with one cloned from my DNA. Almost all the wounds Barry left upon me have faded, except for a light scar on my face from when he ripped my cheek open.

It cost a million dollars to extract the needed elements from Yabechun's blood and synthesize the concoction that was injected into me and the surgeries. It's kind of funny that it already cost a million to train a special forces soldier. I am now a two-million-dollar man.

When Yabechun declares my physical training complete. I am given the task of becoming a trainer myself. "The original plan was to release enhanced recruits back to their countries of origin to test which country could utilize these assets best. Now you will be tasked with turning them into real weapons of war."

I ask Yabechun, "Do they have any prior military training or are we starting from scratch?"

"Basic military training from their prospective countries."

"I'm not an instructor."

He waves away my objection. "You have years of experience in the field. A far more valuable knowledge set." He hands me a drill instructor's handbook and a stack of files. "Just do some reading."

In my old office I read through the files. I need a new chair my enlarged body barely fits in this sad excuse for a chair. Last time I got to be in here was before Barry started his rampage. A burning starts in the tips of my fingers moving up my arms. Before the pain can drift any further I swallow a pill to soothe out my enflamed nerves.

My team consists of four men. From China is a man named Jin, with no last name, who must be an orphan. A man from the United Kingdom named James, nothing special about him either. The one from Russia goes by the name of Igor, and he's got a faded gang tattoo on his hand. Then another America named Hercules, which is apparently his real birth name. Four freaks to train and lead into battle against alien invaders. A challenge I gladly accept.

Right when I start to feel good about this, I receive a message from Victoria. "Come home or I won't."

I'm not a prisoner, so I rush home to find everything has been packed up and she's about to leave. "Vicky!" I call out from the front door, worried I already missed her.

"In here." Says a voice from the kitchen. The worry doesn't leave me.

She sits at the kitchen table with a singular legal document in front of her.

I tower over her, standing at seven feet tall now. "I'm sorry. I was given an opportunity… Look at how strong I am now." I pick up the kitchen fridge with one arm. "My knee is working too. I'm back in one piece again."

She doesn't react. "I don't care how strong you are. I agreed to spend my life with you, not to wait around alone while you disappear for weeks without a word."

After putting the fridge back down, I sit at the table next to her. "What are you talking about? That's exactly what you signed up for. I told you what I was going to do back in high school. I've had several deployments since my enlistment. Don't play that card. What is this really about? Why aren't you happy to see me back in one piece? My knee is as good as new." I kick my foot out and bend my leg repeatedly, showing off its flexibility. "I even have both eyes back."

"Your eyes are supposed to be green." She doesn't see me as she caresses my cheek. "Your skin has lost its tan, and all of your hair is gone. Are you even John?"

I take her hand, so small and fragile. "Do you remember our first date? Not the first time we met, but when I actually asked you out. My grandfather had just left me that Hot Rod. I didn't have much, and I was terrified I would mess up somehow. We went to dinner, and we were so caught up in talking that we missed the movie."

With her head hung down, I can still see a small smile as she says, "They kicked us out to close."

"At that moment, I knew I could spend the rest of my life with you because I could listen to you talk to the end of the world." My hand cupped under her chin, I gently lift her head. "I'm sorry I didn't tell you what they were doing to me. That's the life I chose, what it has to be like for me to work with top secret individuals. But I'm here now, and no matter how complicated what comes next will be, I don't want to lose you." I place my other hand on her stomach. "Or our future."

I have to protect her from the war that is to come. The monsters from beyond our star will not hurt my family.

CHAPTER 10

ANOTHER HOT DAY IN CAIRO, hidding in the shade after another completion of the loop for fuel. Even in the shade, I am still sweating. One of the nighttime mortars took out the basketball court. A small group of people try to pack the hole with sand and glue. Meatball is in the tent reading an old *Playboy* magazine while picking his nose.

Rick sits down next to me. "Another pointless day in paradise, Jason."

"Yeah. Where's Angel?"

Confused, Rick asks, "Who?"

I stand up as a deep feeling in my gut tells me something is wrong. "Where is Angel? I brought him here. I brought all of you here."

A tsunami of thick yellow smoke begins to consume the outpost. "I have to get you out." I grab Rick by his arm, but my grip feels loose. "No, not again!"

He makes a horrible guttural coughing sound as blood fills his lungs.

I try to pull him to safety, but he remains planted in the same spot. Rick's blue eyes pop, spurting out blood before the rest of his body is consumed by the yellow gas. I turn to run just in time to see Luis pointing his rifle at Meatball.

I cry out for him not to do what I know he wants to do. "I told you he wasn't worth it!"

Luis shoots Meatball, splattering his brain matter across the sand. Then he turns to me, his face twisted into an unnatural smile.

The yellow cloud surrounds me. Nowhere left to run.

Angel bursts through the yellow mist. "This is your fault!"

"I didn't know, I swear," I plead to my friend.

Angel raises a knife.

I let out, "Don't!" as he plunges the blade into my left shoulder. I feel the sharp edge pierce my flesh until it pops out of my back.

The pain wakes me from the floor. I have to check my shoulder to see if my wound jumped through time.

There is nothing to indicate I have ever been stabbed. "It didn't happen. None of it ever happened."

What time is it? Without any clocks or natural light, I have no idea how long I've been trapped in here.

I have remained in the same recovery room I first awoke from, for I am assuming over a week. It's just like being back in solitary confinement. This does not scare me. For I, Jason Baker, have spent months alone in confinement. I know how to combat solitude. Granted, my body is weaker than before, but that just means there is more training to do. When my body hits its max for the day, I turn my attention to exercising my mind. I have a new power from my travel through time. I can see a shadow of the future in action. Currently, I can naturally see a fraction of a second into the future.

My only interactions with people are when I am brought food and a nurse checks my vitals. Not much time to gather information, so I use my food to conduct experiments. Balancing my utensils on the edge of a counter, I focus my mind to anticipate when the spoon will fall. After many tests, I can see almost four full seconds into the future, but the strain results in a nosebleed.

I checked all the cabinets in this examination room the second I was left alone. There wasn't much, most of them were empty. Only one cabinet had anything of use, a jar of cotton swabs, another of popsicle sticks, some bandaging tape, and a nursing school textbook printed in 2002. I'm going to guess someone forgot that after changing posts.

My mind keeps going through memories, trying to pinpoint where I know that guy with red eyes from. I've never met anyone with red eyes like those, closer to animal eyes than human. There was just something about him that seemed so familiar. There are so many memories mashed together in my head though, I can't tell which life he is from. I am forced to trust he will lead me to Angel.

Contained in an unknown government building somewhere on Earth, I read through the nursing textbook to kill time. It's so dry I can read an entire page, then realize I did not understand any of it. I turn the page to a picture of someone with a broken leg, immediately transferring me back to Baghdad where I can see the exact same injury on a fellow soldier as he squirms in pain. I slam the book shut.

"The war didn't happen," I whisper, trying to calm

myself. "The war never happened." I try to slow my breathing. "Everyone is safe."

Maybe I should try to access the computer that doctor was working on earlier. I try the classic passwords from my time in the army. Failing five times before I am locked out. It was worth a shot.

Back to working out, I hit my max and collapse to the ground after barely reaching ten pushups. Sweating and breathing hard, I sit back against the wall. I have truly become weak.

CHAPTER 11

OLD FRIENDS

"**M**r. Baker, I see you have been quite active," says the doctor with the bad comb-over as he checks my vitals.

I say, "Yeah, you guys didn't give me much else to do."

The doctor says, "Really? I was informed you were provided entertainment while I was attending to my other duties." He turns to the man in uniform that punched me. "Did you not provide him with anything?"

Stoic, the man says, "No, on surveillance he seemed quite entertained."

I glance at the camera overlooking my bed. There's no bathroom, just a standalone toilet that gets changed out when the nurse brings me food. Either he's a creep or a master at doing the minimum. I bet he's someone that hates his job and looks for any means to not work.

The doctor continues, "Anyways, I have been informed that you will be joining your friend today." He makes a grimace as he gets a whiff of my body odor. "After you are cleaned up."

I am surprisingly used to this smell. In juvey, I would spend months in solitary with nothing more than intense workouts to occupy my time. For a secret military facility, they are lacking in the basic needs department. Is there just so much red tape to maintain secrecy that they forgot the basics? Typical military grade bullshit. Career bureaucrats at the top while the rest is run by kids fresh out of high school. I should know. I was put in charge of an entire platoon at nineteen. I didn't know anything useful.

After a shower in a large locker room and a clean pair of military scrubs, I am taken by wheelchair though many winding hallways. The doctor leaves me with the guard when we reach an elevator. He has other duties today apparently. After a long elevator ride, we arrive at what appears to be an aircraft hangar converted into a manufacturing facility. More than a hundred people are working on strange circular devices of various sizes. There is no sign of natural light, only more fluorescent light and workers have individual lamps. They don't look to be military personnel based upon their clothing. Their shirts aren't even tucked in.

All this movement makes my head ache, blurring my vision. We stop at the bottom of a metal staircase that leads to a second story walkway with an enclosed room overlooking production.

I say jokingly, "I guess this place wasn't built handicap accessible."

My guard remains silent.

"Not even a smile?" I stand up. "Just be ready to catch me if I fall. My legs are a bit wobbly." A lie, my legs can handle this, but they don't need to know that. Got to play weak for now.

By the time I reach the second-floor walkway, I play up my legs trembling. "Did you bring the wheelchair up?" I quip, leaning my weight against the railing.

We both look down at the wheelchair at the bottom of the stairs.

"You can go get it. I'll wait."

My guard gives no indication that he plans to get it, then says, "No one will steal it."

If I had the strength, I would strangle him. Instead, I say, "Just lead the way, Stone or would moron be better?"

He spits out, "It's Stevenson."

"Thank you, Stevenson. I still think you're a moron."

Stevenson pulls me from the railing, almost dragging me to the only room at the top of the stairs. Another man in military camouflage blocks the door. Stevenson and the other man exchange a formal salute. "I have brought this one for his day of work with your prisoner."

The other guard says, "Understood." Then with a knock, he opens the door.

I pull myself out of Stevenson's grip to walk in by my own strength.

The room is a bit bigger than mine. Another guard sits in the far back of the room reading a book. Angel sits at a desk, throwing a tennis ball through a metal circular mirror and then catching the ball as it bounces out of an adjacent circle. He repeats the action over and over, not caring how strange that looks.

Did he make a handheld wormhole? "Angel?"

He stops, letting the ball bounce out of the portal un-impeded, then slowly turns in his chair to me for the first time in years. From above dark bags, his eyes see through me. Teeth are still crooked, but I'm glad he still has them all. His skin is a bit lighter, from lack of sun most likely. Not the Hispanic delinquent he left Juvey as, he's now an emaciated scientist, white lab coat and all.

Stevenson leaves Angel and I with the man reading in the back. We don't say anything for a long time, just staring at each other. I feel tension in the air, but I am overjoyed to see my friend alive and mostly well.

I'm the one to break the silence. "You did it."

He says, "I did."

I ask, "How? I only gave you formulas from my travels through time. How did you make a teleporter?"

"Trial and error. I call it Angel's Window." There is an underlying emotion in his voice.

"It looks like it functions more as a wormhole. Shouldn't it be called Angel's Doorway?"

He says, "It's called Angels Window."

His muscles tensed the moment he looked at me. It's too strong to be mere anger, there's hatred in him.

"What happened to you?"

His neck stiffens. "A lot happened to me." He smiles. "I'm glad you're not dead." His smile is more deranged than happy.

"Turns out my tumor was misdiagnosed. They messed me up with meds I didn't need. Then I woke up here. By the way, where is this place?" I rub my new hair growth, acting cool while adjusting my feet to prepare for possible combat. I don't have the strength for a real fight, just need to hold him off until the guard in the back comes to aid.

Angel mumbles through gritted teeth, "Shame." He

spins in his chair, gesturing to the window overlooking the main floor. "This is the legendary Area 51."

So, I'm in the Nevada desert. At least I'm still stateside. Now I need to figure out if I'm underground or just in a really big building. I've heard the stories about this place, same as everyone else. It's kind of cool. I'm now inside the base where they build all the stealth bombers.

Angel continues with a bit of glee, "Where we are building weapons for the great war to conquer the stars."

"What are you talking about? You stopped the war. That was why I gave you the notebook. We passed the day the nukes were meant to fly."

Angel shakes his head. "No, you idiot. Technology doesn't stop war. It only makes it more devastating."

"But the nukes didn't fly. There is no war in this time line."

"Jason, you goddamn fool." He stands up. "There will always be war, pain, and destruction." Grabbing one of the mirrors, he holds it to face me. "This is what you made. Go ahead, put your hand in it."

I hesitate, looking into my shadowy future for the next three seconds. Other than worsening my headache, I don't see any danger despite feeling it. My hand passes through with no resistance. I can feel the wooden desk while I stand three feet away.

Quickly retracting my hand, I say, "That's incredible. How is it powered?"

Angel shows me the intricate wiring of the device, which seems quite delicate. The battery is of non-terrestrial origin apparently. The smaller the portal, the less power needed.

Other scientists have developed a dual battery design so it can change power resources without turning off.

"As long as the portal stay on, it can transfer matter any distance." Angel turns to the guard, "Jeb, can I do the thing?"

Jeb closes his book, straightening up in his seat. "Fine, just don't spin me this time."

Angel hands Jeb one of the portals.

Jeb slides his head through until it pops out the portal on the other side of the room. "Tada!"

Angel grabs the portal with Jeb's head sticking out. "It's like a magic trick." Then he rips out the battery.

The portal closes, slicing Jeb's head clear from his shoulders.

"Real magic."

Jeb's body slumps down in his chair as blood spurts onto his book.

The shock immediately makes me jump back. I should have looked into the future. "Why did you do that?"

Angel drops the powered off device to the ground next to Jeb's head. "I didn't want interference." He takes out a sharpened piece of metal with a taped handle. "Don't bother with the door. It's locked, and they only open it for Jeb no matter how much I scream."

I raise my fists, focusing my mind to see his first strike. In this weakened state, my new sight is my best defense.

Angel steps just out of striking range. "You cost me my family. My mother Gloria Luna Cortez, my half-sister Rosa Martinez, my baby brother Gabriel Luna Martinez, and the closest thing to a real father, Francisco Martinez. I'm going to carve their names into your flesh. Before I kill you."

My eyes focus on the incoming threat. "How did I cost you anything? I didn't know what kind of technology would be created or how it would be used. All that mattered was stopping the cycle. My mind was being shattered every time a new timeline was created. You shifted the paradigm."

"Enough of your stupid speeches!"

I can see he's going to strike with a stab to my gut. As he lunges in, I push the blade aside and retaliate with a palm strike to his nose. My strikes are not what they used to be. Angel swings the blade back, barely missing me. I grab his arm to gain control of the weapon. His free hand then grabs my neck. I try to pull back but trip on Jeb's severed head, causing us both to fall to the floor. Angel's grip tightens around my throat, and he points the blade down at me. I can feel my strength fail as we fall to the ground, yet out of my pure will to live, I stop the blade an inch from my chest.

Focusing my brain to see into the future in a desperate attempt for a way out, I only see images of a bloody fight in Baghdad flash in front of me. I shove my thumb into Angel's right eye, but he doesn't yield.

Pushing down harder, he screams, "You took everything from me!" His unyielding hatred thirsts for my blood.

With his full body weight leaning on the blade, it begins to enter my flesh at my left shoulder. Every life connects to this one as my mind strains to the source of all my pain.

I yell out a desperate, high-pitched squeal, "Get off!" as my will to live overrides all my senses, pulling from a strength far greater than anything I've ever felt before flowing through me.

The energy releases, hurling Angel across the room. He

hits the wall with a loud metallic thud and with only one eye, looks at me in disbelief.

Nothing matters any more. All unneeded thoughts leave me once again, just as they did in all the other lives, leaving me armed with only the primal will to survive.

The locked door breaks off its hinges as I push my way through. The door guard and Stevenson are thrust from the second-floor walkway. They don't matter anymore. The engineers sound alarms as my body moves down the stairs. Guns drawn, military police rush in through an open door to a dim desert. With a wave of my hand, they are sent into the air. I pick up one of the Berettas they dropped.

I feel the light of the setting sun upon my skin for the first time in this life. Gun shots ring out, but nothing touches me. From the depths of my soul, I scream, "Leave me alone!" and a shock wave pushes everything away, warping the metal of the hangar behind me.

Memories of my desert home return. *I am Jason Baker of Yuma.*

The power fades from me, and I notice a large amount of blood on my shirt, from my nose. "Oh no, what did I just do?" My sight blurs as I drop to my knees, heart racing. I try to catch my breath, but I feel my heart burning.

People are yelling as I fall to my back, now seeing only a bright light above me.

CHAPTER 12

NON-TERRESTRIAL

YOU'RE NOT DONE YET, *JASON*.

The sound of daytime TV pulls me back to this reality. My eyes open to an unfamiliar metal environment. I hear voices but not with my ears.

"He's not one of us!"

"But he let out a yell from The Source."

"No primate has a connection to The Source anymore. We should dump him and return to our mission. It's a leaking biohazard."

I struggle to sit up, holding my throbbing head. Feels as though my brain is trying to break out of my skull. "What are you guys talking about?"

There are two short gray-skin humanoid creatures with large heads on the other side of the room. They're wearing tight red and tan jumpsuits that show off thick muscles of odd shapes. I count several items of chrome metal on their utility belts. Their large black eyes have a slight red iris focused on me. I would scream in horror, but I don't have the strength to do much of anything.

The strangest thing is that my eyes are drawn to a wall where a TV drama show is projected. My sister used to follow this exact show religiously. I can't remember the name. It's not important, but why are these creatures watching bad TV?

Its jaw unmoving, one of them says, "It dares to speak to us?"

The other argues, "It has accessed The Source. It needs to be examined before exterminated."

I don't like the sound of that. Where did my gun go? The Beretta is right next to me, but as I attempt to aim it at my abductors, one of the creatures points a long finger in my direction. An invisible hand rips my gun away as an unseen weight pins me to the ground. I hear its condescending thoughts, *"A primitive weapon."*

The room jolts violently to one side, tossing all of us. *Are we falling?*

I grab onto what was the floor as we begin to spin. I can see an incoming impact as I strain my mind once again. My head throbs with pain, stopping me from seeing any further.

One of the creatures demands, "How did you access The Source?"

I am unable to reply as everything goes dark once again, but I hear it say, "It must survive to tell."

There is a feeling of weightlessness as the patterns of time flow past me as they always have before my eyes open to the real world. The stars sparkle in the night sky. Every part of my body aches as I lay in the desert sand. I can hear a helicopter coming. There is the smell of smoke nearby.

Which desert am I in?

I don't have any equipment, wearing only scrubs covered

in dried blood. There is a circular craft roughly the size of an SUV less than fifty feet from me. How the hell did I just survive a crash in that thing? One of the aliens drags out its companions that have been badly hurt. Blue blood drips from an open chest wound. I scramble behind some nearby brush, concealing myself from what is to come. My head throbs as the creature lets out a horrific scream. This makes my brain feel as though it is bleeding. An Apache helicopter turns on a spotlight, illuminating the crash site while multiple military jeeps of armed soldiers make a perimeter. They stand almost right next to me, and I hesitate to breathe.

Please just keep your focus on the aliens.

From a speaker, someone orders in a southern accent, "Stand down. This is your only warning."

Four of the silver metallic tubes float from the uninjured alien's belt. They begin to emit a slight hum as each extends into long pointed blades. Burning a red glow, they begin to spin. Without speaking, the alien screams into all of our minds, *"Filthy primates!"* Then it sends two of the blades spinning into the surrounding soldiers while another blade splits the helicopter right down the middle. The final blade spins around the alien at high-speed like a helicopter blade, creating a protective shield as the alien holds its injured comrade in its arms, deflecting incoming bullets.

Chaos erupts in the desert.

I hold my ears, having forgotten how loud close-range gunfire is.

Large soldiers move unnaturally fast while firing at the alien. One of the blades spins just above me, chopping a nearby soldier in half. Rather than cowering, I go to the divided man and scavenge for anything useful. I immediately take his helmet, not sure how much help it is in this situation but thinking it's better than nothing. The blade cut through his rifle without resistance. Before slowly crawling away, I take his camel pack of, hopefully, water.

Someone yells, "Enough!"

I look back to see that man with red eyes spiriting toward the alien at Mach speed.

The alien screams in hatred, "Abomination!"

With the impact of artillery hitting flesh, the man with red eyes lands a punch to the alien creature, sending its limp body to splatter against the crashed craft. All the blades retract into their handles while losing direction and continue their trajectories into the ground, one of them landing not far from me. A plain silver metallic cylinder. I don't even contemplate as I instinctively pick one up, taking it as my own.

With one alien reduced to paste, the man with red eyes turns his attention to the alien injured in the crash. "Where is my human?"

It speaks in broken English, "One, with the…Source. You failed."

The man with red eyes examines a slash on his left side. The red blade cut straight through his body. He should be dead but instead brushes it off as he shouts out orders. "Bring in the cleanup crews. I want this craft fixed up and ready for flight. And take this one back to base for biological testing."

People in hazmat suits grab the injured alien.

"It will be a good test subject for our latest rabies strain."

Having seen too much, I slip away into the desert before they search my way.

CHAPTER 13

NON-TERRESTRIAL ATTACK

"CAPTAIN KANE, THE BASE HAS been attacked!" yells some Private in the military police.

I respond, "Again?" feeling dread mixed with a bit of annoyance. My brother just shot up this place two months ago. "How is it that the most remote top-secret base in the country keeps getting attacked?"

Still in a panic, the private says, "I don't know, sir. These were extraterrestrial."

That brightens my spirit a bit. "Load up, men!"

My squad of enhanced soldiers put on Kevlar vests that are a bit small on our large forms, load up with all the ammo we can carry, and run out after the private. We reach the hangar, quickly outpacing the little MP. Several stealth aircraft take off into the darkening sky. At the hangar, we find the door has been blown outward, but there are no scorch marks. Even stranger the frame around the door is indented inward. My men quickly secure the area. I find the person in charge of the building, an engineer under military contract.

"What happened?"

He says, "I don't know. Some teenager just sent those men in the air by just waving! Then the freaking door flew open. What else are you freaks making here?" He points to two bodies of MPs crumpled by extreme blunt force trauma.

Next to me, Hercules asks, "How?"

"Like I said, I don't know! He just kind of waved at them and they went flying."

Before I can process, a Humvee drives up with more military police. A seasoned sergeant says, "Captain Johnathan Kane, alien aircraft has been shot down. I was told to collect you to secure the crash site."

I order Hercules, "Secure the hangar. Find out everything that happened here. Everyone else roll out."

As we drive through the bumpy desert, far from any road, I ask the sergeant, "Any idea what we're going to be fighting?"

The sergeant says, "Not sure. I have just as much information as you. Most of the time, Yabechun is the first one on sight to neutralize alien threats."

Jin asks, "Where is our great leader now?"

"Flying back from New York. He had to give an address at the United Nations."

"So, we get to be the first people to lay the smack down on ET," Igor says with a smile. "This is going to be fun. Ain't that right, James?"

Unmoving, James has kept his head pointed forward the entire drive, refusing to answer anyone. He seems more of the silent type than the closet psycho.

The sergeant says, "Their craft was spotted by the hanger right after the attack. Our own aircraft took off in pursuit.

My superior told me to grab the enhanced soldiers before going to the crash site."

Jin asks, "How did they take it down?"

The sergeant says, "I don't know. I'm just a glorified security guard. They don't tell me what is built. Clearly something beyond my pay grade."

James finally says, "There's a green flame," pointing to a strange glow in the distance.

The sergeant notifies all other troops in the area of the green fire. Everyone approaches the downed spacecraft, ten vehicles of troops, including us and an Apache helicopter as air support surround the site.

The spacecraft is a dark metallic plate with a football shaped center illuminated by a green flame. The sun has set, but each of the Humvees shine flood lights onto the site, where one gray humanoid with no hair and an abnormally large head in a red and tan jumpsuit stands holding a second gray humanoid in its two arms. The injured alien bleeds blue liquid from its chest.

For all I know, I am the first human being to speak to these creatures. I have to represent not only my own family but the military as a whole at this moment. With weapons hot, I yell, "Stand down! This is your only warning." *Good choice of words. Threatening and not insulting. Just to the point.*

The uninjured alien yells, *"Filthy primates!"* without opening its mouth as four long, glowing red swords shoot out at us. I drop to the ground as the blade slices clean through the MP sergeant. I open fire with my M249 light machine gun on the two creatures as the Apache Helicopter is split down the middle, causing it to come crashing to the ground. Every bullet fired from me or anyone else is blocked by a sword spinning around the alien while the other blades cut through armored troops like a hot knife through butter. We need a new strategy.

Jin and Igor create a crossfire as they use their enhanced speed running around the alien to find a gap in its protection. James slides in the sand to land right next to me as one of the spinning blades just misses him.

"Where did you go?"

James hands me a bag. "Grenades, sir."

"Good find." I take two.

I move away from James. He pulls the pin on one and tosses the explosive. It freezes in midair before flying right back at James. He jumps behind a Humvee just as it detonates.

"Cook it first!" The enemy clearly has telekinetic abilities and even if it didn't, returning a grenade to the sender is an easy means of defense.

I pull the pin, reach back and count. One, two…on three, one of the blades spins right past me, cutting down a nearby soldier. I throw, but my momentum is off as only a stump of my arm remains. I look back to see my severed limb on the ground with the grenade still in hand. Instinctively, I dive away as the small bomb explodes, sending me crashing to the ground. I don't lose consciousness, but I feel dazed. I'm definitely hurt, but I'm not sure how much damage there is. First, I check my sack, finding everything is still there but my right arm was cut off just below the elbow. It's not bleeding, looks like it was cauterized as it was severed. My Kevlar vest took most of the shrapnel damage. Blood pools in the sand from my legs. If this is the end, I'm taking the enemy with me.

With my rifle awkwardly in my left arm, I empty the remains of my magazine. "Die, motherfucker!"

It blocks every bullet. I swear it smiles at my inability to hurt it.

James hurls half a jeep at the alien, only to have it deflected. "Just die already!"

Even with my damaged hearing from the grenade, I hear someone yell, "Enough!"

I see Yabechun running in a full sprint, kicking up the desert into a storm behind him. I've only ever seen jets move as fast as him.

The alien screams in hatred, "Abomination!"

Yabechun breaks through the alien's defense, landing a punch that breaks the sound barrier and splatters the alien against the crashed ship in a blackened paste. The sand catches up to him, spraying everyone. Yabechun shakes out his hand before turning his attention to the alien with the large chest wound. "Where's my human?"

It speaks, sucking in air, "One, with the…Source. You failed."

He leans in close, whispering just loud enough for me to eavesdrop. "Failures breed success." He stands back up brushing off his side where one of the blades cut clear through his body. "Bring in the cleanup crews. I want this craft fixed up and ready for flight. And take this one back to base for biological testing."

People in hazmat suits grab the alien.

"It will be a good test subject for our latest rabies strain."

When did the hazmat team get here?

Yabechun looks straight at me. "What happened to you?"

My adrenaline starts to fade away, allowing me to feel pain again. "Hit with my own grenade. Looks like it got you too."

There is a deep cut right where his liver would be. Yabechun brushes it off, not caring for the fatal injury. "The price of immortality," he jokes. "It hurt less than jumping out of my plane to get here in time."

I look back to try and find my arm. James is holding what was one of my fingers for me to see. "I don't think this can be reattached, sir."

Yabechun shakes his head with disappointment. "Where's the Evac? And somebody get me a phone. I left mine on the plane. Hollywood has a lot of work to do. Going to need something good to keep the enemy distracted."

At the hospital, they remove shrapnel from my legs sewing many stitches. Plus, I get some new mechanical implants in the nub of my shortened limb. This new body heals quickly.

Then I am brought to Yabechun's office with the rest of my squadron, probably so he can berate us over the failed mission. If only I didn't lose my arm, maybe things could have gone better. No, I have to remember what my father taught me. *Never give an excuse to your mistakes, just own it.* I say, "Sir, I would like to apologize for my failure as the commanding officer. I should have organized the men better to neutralize the threat."

Yabechun responds, "Calm down, John. This is a debrief, not a trial. Hell, I'm impressed none of you are dead after direct contact with a threat using superior weaponry. Proof your enhancements work. The MPs suffered thirty losses. It's going to take some time to get replacements."

I share a look of confusion with my men. "Really? It was a disaster, and I lost an arm."

He brushes that off with a wave of his hand. "We have robotics that can fix your situation. Don't underestimate what I have at my disposal." He presses a button under his desk that covers the large window behind him with metal shades. "And don't let those deaths weigh upon you. There will be far more losses in the war to come. Now, Hercules, please share with everyone what happened at the production hangar that caused all of this?"

Hercules straightens up his posture. "Sir, from what I was able to gather, a prisoner, young sickly looking teenage boy, was brought to the creator of portal technology to work with him."

Yabechun says, "You can use their names. All of you have clearance."

"Sorry, sir. The creator...I mean, Angel Molina and the guard inside the room were caught off guard when Jason attacked them with an unknown ability. Something close to telekinesis, this attack threw Angel across the room and cut off the guard's head. Jason used his new power to kill all the guards outside the room protecting the classified project. Once outside, a bright light pulled him into the air, which we now know to be the alien craft."

Yabechun asks, "What did Angel say about his friend when questioned?"

"That the power came out of nowhere. He only saw some of it as he lost an eye in the outburst."

Yabechun thanks Hercules before addressing us. "I'll deal with Angel tonight. Jason Baker is the original creator of portal technology. And he was unaccounted for at the crash site. This means one of two things. Jason was either abducted in a second ship that got away or he's somewhere in the desert. Either way, we cannot take the chance of our enemy gaining this technology. We will have to strike hard and fast if we want any chance at victory."

Igor speaks up, "Then we're going to need something better than pea shooters. Nothing we shot had any effect against just one of those fuckers. We are grossly out gunned against an army of them. Unless you plan to kill them all by yourself."

"Excellent point, Igor." He stands up. "Now, as some of you should have realized by now, I am not built like the average person. Hercules, please hold out your arm for me."

Hercules obliges.

Yabechun grabs the young man's hand, locking his grip. "Now push as hard as you can."

Hercules does as ordered.

Yabechun lets his arm bend back. "I'm using the bare minimum of my strength, equal to the average person. With the power I have given you, you are easily able to push back. However…"

Suddenly Hercules starts to get pressed back and struggles to push all of his strength forward but is still driven back.

"I have gained strength from over twelve thousand years of life on this planet, suffering pain on a scale incomprehensible to your simple minds." Once Hercules's hand touches the ground, Yabechun relents. "Now, I cannot be everywhere at once. That is why each of you were gifted with a fraction of my strength. You four will be on the front lines of this conflict, leading our people to victory." He helps Hercules back to his feet. "Follow me."

Yabechun brings us to an armory and hands me a combat vest. "These are going to be the new standard issue for infantry troops. It's as light as plastic but can stop a rifle bullet as large as a 7.62mm round."

It has a thick plate across the chest and scaling wraps around the gut for movement with an additional plate hanging down to cover the jewels between the legs.

"They are easy to maneuver in and simple to put on, but most importantly cheap. They are currently in mass production worldwide. This is the United States' model. Other countries are trying to come up with their own unique design. The important part is the ballistic plate. Steel will stop a bullet but is heavy, and Kevlar is too pricey for the bureaucrats. A scientist figured out a new way to make plastic that results in a product twice as strong as steel, with none of the weight. The fool only wanted to use it for transportation. He freaked out when we used it for weapon's testing."

He brings us to a full body suit of armor that somehow looks both sleek and bulky at the same time. "This is your new uniform. A highly advanced suit of armor. The armor covers almost everything with breaks at each joint for mobility. Most importantly, sections can be taken off to address wounds or go to the bathroom. The armor is coated with an additional layer of graphene, an extract from graphite that's essentially pure carbon, making this body armor the strongest man-made material on the planet, and one of the most expensive."

I place the helmet over my head. The heads-up display can switch to infrared vision and has an artificial intelligence that tracks suit diagnostics and magazine count, as well as built-in radio communication.

While examining the unique camouflage pattern, I comment, "Will this make me a three-million-dollar man?"

Yabechun presents a robotic arm prosthetic. "Three million five hundred thousand."

"Praise this country's runaway military budget."

Hercules makes an overly sincere salute. "God Bless America."

Yabechun picks up an assault rifle with an odd-looking grenade launcher. "Now follow me to the firing range."

Outside, within the empty desert, Yabechun gives a signal to an artillery team with their M1299 Howitzer pointing at a portal. They load the 155mm shell into the cannon. "The only downside is that this new weapon takes some time to set up on the other end." He points the rifle at a broken van roughly two hundred yards away from us.

The underside grenade launcher opens up the barrel and expands to about a foot wide. Yabechun pulls the trigger sending a signal to the artillery team. They fire the self-propelled explosive round speeding out of Yabechun's under barrel portal that destroys the old van, turning it into bits of scrap metal.

"Behold, gentlemen, the true future of warfare."

We stand there in amazement looking for the right words. A hand held Howitzer is beyond what I knew to be possible.

CHAPTER 14

THROUGH NOTHINGNESS

REMEMBER YOUR NAME.

"Jason…Baker."

What is your purpose?

"I don't know?"

What is your purpose?!

"I don't know anymore," I mumble as I walk this neverending desert.

My skin is sunburned, my legs ache, and my head throbs. Everything hurts, and yet I don't know why I keep fighting the will of gravity. Despite the unyielding force pulling me to the ground, to give up, I keep walking. I need to keep going even if there is nothing beyond that horizon other than more desert.

The stolen water has run dry, and I haven't seen any signs of civilization. Maybe I shouldn't have run from the military. Heck, I would flag down anything if it meant water.

There is nothing but endless sand.

My foot slips, sending me to the ground. *Can this finally be my end?*

"What am I now?"

You're not done yet.

My eyes open to the darkened desert with a light in the distance. My muscles strain as I force myself back up. "Come on, you miserable waste of space."

I can hear the cadence from boot camp ringing in my ears.

Mama, Mama, can't you see,

What the army's gone done to me.

They put me in a barber's chair,

Spun me around, I had no hair.

Mama, Mama, can't you see,

What the army's gone done to me.

Mom…

How long has it been since I've seen my own mother? God, I need to get back home. To my family, to the life I lost. *Please just let me get home. I just want to go home.*

As I get closer to the light, I notice it's in fact a small campfire by a retro looking RV. I take the metal cylinder I got from the crash site. I haven't figured out how to activate the blade yet, but I can still use it as a blunt weapon.

I try to be stealthy, but my exhaustion is creating heavy steps. The smell of cooking meat enters my nose. Hunger grips me, and I become more animal than man.

The only person by the fire is an elderly Asian man cooking a hotdog on a long fork. He doesn't look at me. "About time. Please join me." His voice is warm and welcoming.

I freeze, unsure what to do.

The man says, "I've been waiting for you. There is no need to hide."

I enter the light of the fire, suddenly conscious of my blood-stained shirt.

He gestures to an empty seat by the fire with a bottle of water beside it.

There is no ounce of hesitation as I take the water and chug down the lifesaving liquid. I let out a loud burp, feeling much better.

He says, "Please have a seat." Then he hands me the cooked hotdog in a fresh bun.

I take the food without questioning why this old man is showing a blood-stained stranger such kindness.

"Been waiting for you for a while now."

Too busy eating, I don't answer.

"But it's not every day you meet another who has seen The Source of all things."

I pause and look over at him with my mouth full of unchewed food. "Wha…?"

"Yes, I have witnessed The Source as well. That is how I knew to be here. I have seen this night many times. Another like me would come from the desert in need of help."

I swallow down my food. "What the hell are you talking about? What is The Source everyone keeps talking about?"

"It is the origin of all things. The very seed of life. Without such there would be nothing. It stretches and bends to be the never-ending line of time flowing forever. We forget as we grow, only to remember as the physical body fades."

The light from when I traveled through time, what I used to create my formulas. "I saw it when I got hit by a nuclear bomb."

The old man smiles at that. "Same as I."

"Wait, but nuclear weapons were only ever used at the end of World War Two." Then it hits me. "You're Japanese."

He nods his head.

"How old were you when it happened?"

He tosses another log onto the dying fire. "I was ten years old when the bomb dropped on Hiroshima. It sent my mind back three years into the past. I had no idea what happened the first time. Just a light, then pop! I'm seven years old, walking to school. I relived that moment at leas5 six times."

"How did you break the cycle?"

"I ran away. No one would believe a seven-year-old kid about an act from God. Of course, I would eventually find out it was a bomb dropped by the Americans long after the knowledge would have been useful. Are you still stuck in the cycle?"

"No, I broke mine. Stopped the third world war from ever happening."

"Impressive. I wish I could have done that."

"Thanks, but I think it ended up costing me differently. I spent my childhood in prison. All my friends hate me, the government is trying to use me, and I don't know what has become of my family. And there may now be a much worse war on the way."

He places a kettle of water on the fire. "I take it you used what you saw to make a weapon for the government. I didn't try to dissect what I saw scientifically. Instead, I sought out the answers spiritually, met mystics and shamans all over the world who taught me the language of the ancients. The bits of truth hidden within all stories." Steam shoots from the kettle. "Slowly something began to grow, then upon my true awakening, I understood it all." The kettle rises from the fire without anyone touching it.

I try to glance into the future, but my brain feels as though it's hemorrhaging. I fall back into my chair, holding my skull and clenching my teeth against the pain.

The old man calmly says, "You've overtaxed what your mind can understand. If you continue to push this ability, you will cause irreversible damage." The floating kettle pours hot water into two hovering teacups. "A shaman gave me tea brewed from a tree root only found deep in the Amazon. This plant has all but been lost to us. It allowed me to see all I needed to see. Deepening my understanding of what I had unlocked. He warned that using power gained too quickly will result in the abuse of that power and will lead to your own demise."

He floats the teacup over to me. "You must experience death to see The Source of all things by entering into the Void. Then all of time and space will open to you."

I accept the tea and drink the dark hot water. "How long does it take to kick—"

Everything peels away to the fundamental roots of creation.

What exactly was in that tea?

I no longer have a body. I no longer exist. I am no longer Jason. That was the name of someone else's life. Someone who lived long ago and is now just a fading memory.

There is nothing, no light, no sound, only a void.

Why am I here?

The void does not change, only stretches on forever.

Where did it all start for me?

Images appear before me, moments in Jason's life but not where it started.

I look at his ancestors. They will have the answers I seek. I look to the generation before Jason's.

I see his mother's brother walking in the dense jungle of Vietnam. His eyes see far beyond me, into the horizon. A half-smoked cigarette hangs from chapped lips. He is unkempt from a long night patrol. Without warning, he steps on a land mine and vanishes in the explosion.

His uncle was too far gone. I must look farther into the past.

I see his grandfather on a Normandy beach as men are being cut down by machine gun fire. From behind a small sand wall, he shouts for a medic and holds his friend as he bleeds from the neck. No one comes and his friend dies in his arms.

There is so much horror. I don't want to see this.

But I keep being pulled to the wars.

I see a man that looks exactly like Jason but with long greasy hair and a bright red kilt, as he charges an English army with nothing but a wooden shield and a sword. I witness the carnage of old-fashioned war. Covered in mud, his ancestor squeezes the throat of his enemy. The dying man claws with muddy hands, desperate to survive, only to slowly fade into the void.

Jason's ancestor looks at me with my own eyes, those of a killer. "My will to live outweighs yours." With sword in hand, he treks through the mud and continues to fight.

My will to live? I've pushed through everything to survive. Never giving up. Why? Because I just wanted to live? All I ever got for living was more suffering.

Give me a real reason, please.

I see my friends.

Rick is joking with Alex and Zack as they play video games and laugh about pointless things. I wish I could join them.

I am there playing games. This is where I want to be.

Each of them dies. Rick chokes on his own blood. Zack is incinerated by a large ball of fire. Alex is pulled under with the ship, drowning in the cold dark depths of the ocean.

They return to playing games without me. If I didn't stop the war, they would have all died. I had to lose them to save them.

Where is Luis?

He is reading a Criminology textbook in prison with several other Mexican gang members, protected and learning with Angel's cousin David. Without my actions, he would have died pointlessly. His path is his own now.

Why did Angel try to kill me?

I see him with his family, eating dinner in a small home. His mother is feeding his baby brother while Angel tells his sister and stepfather about portal technology. Then fire consumes the house as it fills with horrible cries of anguish and despair after the man with red eyes leaves with my notebook.

Angel lost everything because of my meddling with time. "I'm sorry, my friend. I'm so sorry." But he can't hear me.

I need to know if it was worth it. What does this new future hold? Then I am catapulted forward to a destroyed city. Great structures of humanities ability have been reduced to ruins. I stand alone, facing the man with red eyes as he holds the head of God in his hands.

The vision fades, and I am left once again alone in the void, watching the emptiness expand forever. Unsure of the answers I have been given, I fear I am just an animal trying to stay alive. Same as everyone else. Fighting against the inevitable even though we never asked to be here.

Is that it?

Yes, for all who want to live. The void does not care as it connects to everything. It expands beyond this one moment to the next, for this void is The Source of it all. All moments happen simultaneously, even though I could only see them one at a time. I pull upon the threads of this Source, feeling the energy pass through my mortal body. It takes me back to the moment I pushed Angel away. Now I clearly see the fabrics of reality bend as I access the Source of all things for the first time. Invisible hands from other moments of reality pull Angel from me before tossing him across the room.

Now I see. I'm ready to go home now.

I awaken, still in my chair by the fire, as the old Japanese man sits sipping tea while the sun begins to rise behind him. He asks, "Did you find the answers you seek?"

My headache wanes. "Sort of."

"Then you will find the rest when you are ready." He hands me a piece of toast. As the sun begins to rise on a new day.

CHAPTER 15

THE ROAD HOME

"Easy now, Jason. You can do this," I mumble as I try to pour a shaky cup of water into an empty cup without physically touching it. My brain begins to swell and I see visions of war, the destruction of cities and the ruin of life. The cup over corrects, splashing the contents all over the sink.

"Damn it. Why is this so hard?" I turn to the old Japanese man eating a sandwich at the table. "How do you do it, Mr. Shimizu?"

Mr. Shimizu washes down his meal with some warm tea before calmly replying, "Keep your mind clear from all distractions." The RV steering wheel gently adjusts without anyone in the driver's seat. "You keep diving too deep to move through The Source." He then goes to the driver's seat and grasps the steering wheel. "Try picturing your hands still pouring without touching the cup."

I try again with a full cup. It lifts up fine, but as soon as it hovers, the thing starts to shake. I grab it to steady it.

Mr. Shimizu says, "Cheating will only cheat you."

With a deep breath to calm myself, I let go but imagine I'm still holding the cup. The cup remains stable. I tilt the cup and miss the target. As a reflex, I lift the other cup to catch the water only to realize I'm doing it without physical touch.

In my excitement, I drop both cups in the sink, splashing myself. "I did it!"

Mr. Shimizu says, "Good. Now do it again."

Drying off, I say, "I will, give me a second."

I wander to the front of the RV and lean to look out the front window. "Any idea how far out we are?"

He says, "Six more hours."

"Anyone following us?"

He gives a definitive, "No."

"It's kind of surreal, you know, to actually be going home. It's been so long in both realities." *Almost feels too easy.*

Mr. Shimizu gave me some clean clothes and sandals, and we left everything the military gave me buried in the desert. It feels good to wear normal street clothes for once. Now, I'm not one for style, but tan slacks that barely go down to my knees and a tropical themed button up makes me look like a retiree from a Florida beach. Ironically, that is where Mr. Shimizu has been living for the past ten years.

"What did you see when you first entered the void?"

"Many things." He lifts one hand from the wheel, as a cup of tea floats to each of us. "Every possible life, each one slowly leading me to the truth." After taking a sip he says, "This ability came much later and took me many years to perfect."

The tea is really good. "Why didn't you ever use it for

profit? You could have easily started a cult around yourself or become an unstoppable assassin."

He continues to gently sips his tea. "And that is why you struggle with this power. The ability to see the Source and bend the fabrics of reality is a gift, not a superpower. One does not master a deadly art without learning the discipline to not abuse it." He then has me drive. "Stay on the freeway. I'll be up before we get to your desert." Then he goes to the back to take a nap.

The wheel feels oddly familiar in my hands. I haven't driven since Ciro, when the city got bombed with chlorine gas. Yellow fumes start to drift into the road. My foot starts to press harder on the accelerator.

Mr. Shimizu places his hand on my shoulder. "Just breathe. Your realities are blending."

I take a deep breath, taking in the yellow vapor. Nothing happens, so I take another deep breath. The yellow smoke was just from a dust devil kicking up sand. My trauma made me believe it was something worse.

My heartbeat slows down, and my body relaxes. "I'm good."

Mr. Shimizu lets go of me and returns to the back for his nap.

The drive becomes more mind numbing as time passes with nothing but endless desert sand in the land of no shade. Eventually the radio starts to get stations again.

"Tensions rise as the US and Russia continue to conduct military exercises."

Of course it's on the news.

"This could turn from mere exercises as both China and India practice right on each other's borders. Is China ramping up to claim India territory as it did with Tibet so many years ago. We will have our correspondent, Christopher Martin, on to discuss these implications after this break."

I change the channel to a rock station playing some classic hits, which makes me wonder about the music that was inspired in my original timeline. Now without the war, those songs will never exist. So many songs were inspired by Vietnam. Without the chaos of my war, the music to understand it is now gone. That's a strange thought.

Eventually we pass over the rocky hills surrounding my hometown of Yuma. Everything looks different, yet it's still the same bland desert. New restaurants have opened and stores have changed their signs. From here, I know the way by heart. Even though I never got a driver's license in this timeline, it's a drive I did so many times before my world changed.

I stop the RV at the house I grew up in. It has new coat of bright gray paint. "I don't know if I can do this."

Mr. Shimizu is at the table behind me. "You don't have to, but you *need* to."

"When did you wake up?"

"A while ago."

I adjust my outfit, brushing off nonexistent crumbs. "How do I look?"

"As you need to."

Feeling awkward, I say, "I guess this is goodbye."

He nods his head. "It is for now."

Wanting to say more, I search for a conversation. "What are you going to do now?"

He says, "Go where I am needed."

I step out of the air-conditioned vehicle, getting an instant reminder of the uncomfortable dry heat. *I'm home.*

My parents' cars are in the driveway, along with a new one I don't recognize. At the threshold, I press the doorbell.

Nothing happens.

I put my ear against the door and press the button again. Dad must have disabled the doorbell, so I knock extra loud, then wait until I hear my father grumbling as he approaches.

He opens the door. "The sign says no soliciting!" Then he freezes at the sight of me.

"Hi, Dad. It's been a while."

He looks like he's seen a ghost. "Jason…you died."

Not sure what to do, I shrug. "I kind of did."

I hear my mother yell from the kitchen, "What is taking so long?"

Dad yells back, "Jason's here!"

"What?" She walks up behind my dad. "What did you say?"

"Hi, Mom."

She immediately pulls me in, hugging me tight. "Oh my God."

I hug her back, relishing the warm feeling I have not felt in a lifetime.

She lets go, holding me at a distance and looking me over, not believing her eyes. Then she pulls me back in. I feel Dad's hand upon my head before he finally hugs me, accepting me as real. Tears begin to flow.

I'm finally home.

CHAPTER 16

KANE'S HOME

LAY AWAKE IN BED NEXT to my slumbering wife, look-ing at my Polyurethane hand. *What are you becoming, John?*

We had to get a longer bed for my massive frame. Vicky snuggles next to me, barely able to reach across my chest now. I am a goliath next to her. What the hell is my son going to think when he comes into this world? His father is a massive robotic murder machine.

Damnit, John, you can't think like that. Remember the mission. I will sacrifice every ounce of flesh I have to ensure my family's safety. I have placed my trust in my mission, and there it will remain.

Cooking breakfast is my job when I'm home. It's almost a guarantee that I'll wake up first after years of military drills. This new body requires more nutrition, so I cook the entire carton of eggs. Vicky has been getting weird cravings lately, so I have a few options for her when she wakes up.

Vicky waddles in, her pregnant belly sticking out from her shirt. Her hair is disheveled, but she is still as beautiful as the day we first met. She only gives a slight grunt as a good morning. Unfortunately, she's never been a morning person and I know she's been craving a cup of coffee for months.

I ask, "Do you want a normal person breakfast today or…?" I take out a jar of pickles and a fresh open jar of peanut butter.

She takes the pickles and peanut butter to the living room, leaving me alone to eat in the kitchen. I've never understood her need to watch something while she eats. I want my full attention on the meal in front of me.

Eating has become normal with my new arm. I can't actually feel anything with it, but when I bump it on something I swear it feels real. Something about my brain wanting to believe it's real. I think the official term is Phantom Limb. Even as I use this fork, I can feel the tool in my grasp despite not having any nerves in this combination of metal, plastic, and hard rubber. I'll have to replace the power cell in the forearm tomorrow and give it a charge.

Vicky comes back into the kitchen as I clean the plates. "Your parents should arrive sometime after noon."

My hand tightens, breaking the plate.

Vicky looks at me inquisitorial.

I say, "Sorry, I must have pinched a nerve."

Vicky continues, "The spare bedroom is all set for them. Do you know if Austin is coming?"

"I don't think so. He just finished high school so he probably already enlisted, but I don't know when he's shipping out for Basic. Don't worry about him. He can have the couch. When we were kids, he would get the floor."

Vicky says, "Youngest siblings get the worst sleeping spots."

I'm a bit nervous about my parents coming to stay. The general has a meeting with Yabechun on post, and Mom is going stay with us for a while. My duties take me away a lot, and there is a very real chance I could be deployed when the baby comes. Mom has experience raising three boys, so she'll be much more help than I would be anyway.

This will be the first time I've seen them since my fight with Barry. I haven't even spoken a word to them. Vicky's been the one communicating. They've always gotten along. Her home life was rough, to put it simply, and Mom saw her as the daughter she never had.

Eventually the hour of my dread arrives. My parents pull up in a rented car. They both look shocked at how large I am now. Mom still hugs me all the same. The general puts out his hand for a firm handshake. I grasp it with my robotic limb.

He says, "You two ladies head inside. I need to talk to John man to man." After they go inside, he comments, "That's quite the upgrade you got there."

"Yeah, it's been taking some getting used to."

We both stand in silence for a long time, looking out into the Nevada desert. I don't want to say it and I know he doesn't want to either, so the silence grows.

He breaks first. "I haven't heard from my brother in a while. He didn't cash his disability check last month."

"Do you think Uncle Robert's dead?"

"I don't know. Even when he's on a bender, he always cashes his check, but if he were dead, I would have been informed."

"Yeah…"

The silence stretches between us as the desert around us refuses to fill this gap.

"You know who, told me everything."

"I know." The silence thickens again as I am not sure what more to say.

I finally ask, "What does that mean for us?"

Dad says, "I don't know. I understand why you did what you did, but I don't know if I can forgive you. Your actions hurt your mother in a way she will never recover from. She's been hiding it well, but when she thinks she's alone, I've seen her cry. Our family is cursed to this path. To be born a Kane is to be born a killer."

"I'm not looking for forgiveness."

Silence again.

He finally says, "She doesn't know it was you. Officially, Barry died in an accident while on deployment."

"That's probably best." After a moment, I ask, "When's the funeral?"

"When Austin finishes Basic. We'll spread Barry's ashes in Florida. He always liked that place best."

I think back to our childhood, playing soldiers in the backyard and throwing mud at one another. Absolutely ruined our clothes. Mom made us clean everything by hand in the backyard before we were allowed inside again. "Yeah, that was a good home."

We return to silence for a while, until Mom calls us inside where she proceeds to give Vicky and I every single bit of knowledge she has gained as a mother. She even gives Vicky a handwritten notebook of useful tips, every page filled front to back.

Vicky says, "Wow, Susan, you could publish this thing."

Mom waves it off. "Oh, I'm sure I forgot something."

I think she's doing everything she can to not think about Barry. She probably came to terms with the possibility of losing one of us. That's just the nature of our path in life, but that still didn't mean it hurt any less to lose a child.

CHAPTER 17

UNDERDOGS

"T ELL ME, JOHN. HOW WOULD you fight against a superior enemy?" Yabechun asks from behind his desk.

Is this really what he called me in for? He cut short my training with my new Advanced Warfare Suit, not to mention getting used to my new mechanical arm. I've reduced the delay for pulling the trigger, but it's still awkward to use for small, intricate tasks such as washing my hands. I appreciate that the hand is waterproof, but it's still hard plastic with rubber fingertips. I accidentally pulled off a fingernail last night.

General Kane says, "Any day now, son."

This is clearly a test they both concocted. Alright, I'll play along. "I suppose the best way to fight a superior opponent is to fight harder, but it depends on the context. Outside of an arena, fighting dirty is always a safe bet."

Smiling his perfect white teeth, Yabechun says, "You are correct, because the only rule in combat is that there are no rules. A normal person can't fight a grizzly bear in hand-to-hand combat, but with the right tools, the bear quickly becomes prey. Now, how would a military with the technology equivalent to the First World War face a modern twenty-first century fully mechanized military."

That's a hard fight. Bolt action rifles up against fully automatic assault rifles are hardly a challenge. Wooden aircraft stand zero chance against supersonic jets. That being said, it would be a difficult target to hit. Biplanes move so slow they would barely be picked up on modern hardware. I doubt those old engines even produce enough heat to be targeted by heat seeking missiles. Now that I think about it, the rifles in World War I shot thirty odd six rounds, basically arming the entire infantry with high caliber sniper rifles. Not to mention there were no rules back then, and chemical weapons were used freely.

Finally, I say, "The modern military would be caught off guard, unprepared for the lack of tech. And if the old-fashioned military switched to guerrilla tactics, like the Vietcong did in Vietnam, they could stand a chance… But ultimately, I believe the modern military would overpower them."

General Kane nods in agreement. "Yes, so the ones who fell behind would have to strike first and hard enough that the enemy has no time to rally."

"So what is the official plan to fight the alien menace?" I say, wanting to cut through the rhetorical questions.

"Your family never wants to ramble." Yabechun shakes his head in mock disappointment. "The plan is to negotiate. A deal for peace in return for the portal technology."

"I call, bullshit."

"Precisely. Our enemy doesn't truly understand lies." Yabechun's perfect teeth are on display again. "They live in a utopian society that hasn't endured any form of suffering in millenniums. I've already sent a ship to negotiate a prisoner release as a distraction to plant portals for staging."

"What prisoners, sir?"

Yabechun turns the computer monitor on his desk around, revealing a list of a thousand prisoner numbers with experiment details in an excel document. "As our laws dictate, we arrest criminals for kidnapping, murder, and sexual crimes. As they are not humans, they have no rights on my planet, so they receive max sentences without a trial. And as the war they started never truly ended, they are war prisoners subject to enhanced interrogation."

I want to say, "That's a nice way of saying we've captured and tortured aliens," but I don't want to interrupt him.

"With their confessions and the collaborated intel gathered from their home world, we know all points of strategic interest."

I say, "What will the enemy say to your treatment of their people?"

General Kane says, "They've been trying to free their people for years. Small extraction squads flying around the solar system, waiting for an opportunity. That's who took your arm."

That thing clearly had combat training. Precise tactics that targeted the greatest threats first, like cutting down the helicopter first.

Yabechun continues, "While my diplomat sets up the portals for me to travel to their home world, we have already released several infected prisoners into highly populated areas. As I deal with the ruling counsel, the invasion will begin."

I ask, "Infected? How do you infect an alien species?"

"With years of trial and error. As I said, we have captured a thousand of those gray monsters trying to take my people. Unfortunately, not enough to truly persuade them to stop. Now tell me what ailments do you know that can jump species?"

Again, he's making me think instead of just telling me. "I know there was an issue a few years back when the flu infected a bunch of pigs."

"Any others?" General Kane asks.

A little annoyed, I say, "I don't know, sir. I didn't do well in high school biology."

Yabechun continues, "Most of the human race is already infected with the flu, and it mutates every year in the winter, bringing about a good-sized death toll. It can jump species in the right environment. That keeps our enemy away in the cold months. However, I have found rabies to work the best. A guaranteed death and a high likelihood of spreading. Among one of the many things learned from Unit 731 in Ping Fan, during the Second World War. Biowarfare is almost useless unless there are…other side effects. I found a particular strain of Rabies creates extreme fits of madness in the Anunnaki in less than a day after exposure and will lead to infecting another. There is no cure once any of the symptoms emerge, creating roughly a twenty-four-hour window where an infected Anunnaki is driven into a feral madness before dying."

General Kane says, "That's why humans have to get the vaccine immediately after being bitten. And still, it's thirty shots to the gut with long needles."

Finishing their drawn-out speeches, I say, "So we attack while they're distracted."

"Not we. You."

"Me?" I'm shocked at the honor.

"You will lead the ground forces on invasion day, as will the rest of your enhanced team in key locations. I need my best weapons in the fight, preparing the area for aircraft to launch through the portal and nuke key locations." He stands up from behind his modest desk. "Soon we shall bring ruin to their world as they did to ours all those years ago."

The joy in his voice would worry a civilian but not me. I like the idea of leading a fight.

"But the most important aspect of winning a fight against any opponent is that you need a reason to fight. And there is no greater reason than hatred." He looks at his watch. "Speaking of which, you're needed on the tarmac. You have a fight in Detroit to win."

CHAPTER 18

REUNION

"**W**ELL, JASON, YOU FINALLY GOT what you always wanted. Now what?" I say aloud in the empty house.

I had a grand reunion with my parents and siblings and tears were shed as I recounted an exaggerated escape and demonstrated my new powers. I left out the alien weapon I stole, wanting to figure out how it works before sharing. Then they went back to their lives, leaving me alone once again.

My parents left for work and my two older siblings are in college. In my mind, I thought they would have graduated by now, but according to this timeline, they're only college juniors. I'm not complaining. It's great to see my family again. I just thought it would be more. Can't have much of a celebration for my return with possible government agencies after me. It just feels too quiet now.

Looking at my bowl of increasingly soggy cereal, I don't know what to do. I'm a legally dead delinquent on the run from the government. Can't exactly go back to school or apply for a normal job. My knowledge is only on how to survive, whether that is in war or prison. Maybe I can find work as a day laborer out in front of the Home Depot.

I need to get out of here.

I pour the soggy flakes into the garbage disposal. Then with a bottle of water and a pocket full of sugary cornflakes, I walk out the door.

There is another place I need to be. I never got a car in this reality, so I borrow my father's bike. It is only a few miles to the trailhead and another several miles up to the top. Not nearly as difficult as aimlessly wandering the desert or the ruck marches in the army. Yuma doesn't have real mountains, just large rocky hills that barely change elevation. In no time at all, I'm at the cliff side, overlooking the city.

The last time I stood here was with all my friends before we shipped out for the war. What was it we all took a shot of? Snakebite. That's what Zack called it.

I lift my water bottle in reverence. "To a brave new world!" Taking a sip, I sit down in the dirt. "What the hell am I now?" Taking out a small handful of cornflakes, floating them one by one into my mouth. Like watching an imaginary hand feed me. A great power, but I have no idea what to do with it. Any real applications would expose me. Arguably doing this in the open is stupid, but it feels good to practice it. Reminds me all of this is real.

I relax my new power as a jogger comes up the trail. Expecting her to just run past, I give a wave and a "Mornin'," with a mouth full of dry cereal.

She slides to a stop before turning around. "Jason?" She takes off her sunglasses to get a clear view of me. "Jason Baker?"

I swallow my snack before replying, "Maybe…"

She gets right in my face. "I heard you died in prison."

Unsure of how to respond, I give a shrug and an apologetic smile. Then I realize who she is. "Amy?" Then I stop myself from saying more, knowing most of my memories of her are of another timeline. She was the one who held onto me in the bunker when North Korea fired the nukes. I wonder if she ended up with the same guy in this reality.

Her arms wrap around me in an impulsive hug. I freeze, not wanting to strike in defense. She says, "It *is* you! I remember the day you knocked out Dylan's teeth. I was on your side—he was a real ass. Did you know he would purposefully fall into me just to grab my chest, but he stopped after you knocked him good."

I pat her on the back, not returning the hug. "I'm glad some good came of that." I don't have a lot of experience with positive affection.

She lets go of me. "But how are you back? No, don't tell me now. What are you doing later?"

"Not much of anything."

"You need to come to my house tonight. I was going to have a get-together with some friends, and you need to come. Give me your number. I'll text you the address."

Instinctively, I reach for my phone as if I'm back in high school, but I didn't go to high school this time around. "I'm kind of off the grid. Call my parents' home phone. I'll find my way there." Should I warn her not to speak my name over the phone? Maybe, but it will be a good test to see if the government is actually looking for me. They never contacted my parents after I escaped. Maybe they wanted me to escape.

"Okay, I will. You're going to have to tell us how you're

back." She then runs back the way she came with new enthusiasm.

"I'm going to need to come up with a good lie about my past," I mumble to myself.

That night, Dad lets me borrow his car. As I leave, he asks, "Do you think this is a good idea?"

"Honestly, I don't know, but I can't just hide at home forever."

"Not what I meant. You never got a license. I don't want my car wrecked."

I know he's just joking. "I told you all about my time travels. Nothing will happen to your car. And if men in black suits come knocking, you can say it was stolen." Then I float the keys from his hand, across the garage to mine. "I'll be careful."

With printed-out directions from my parents' computer, I find my destination. This feels surreal. Everything is right where it was when I was deployed. Gotta remind myself that wasn't in this timeline and that my grade just graduated high school.

The house is in the nicest part of town. I think Amy's parents are lawyers or something rich like that. This house is extravagant, yet oddly familiar. This is the house my brother took me to when I was younger, the party where the cops showed up. Where Rick and I escaped into the wash, and I ran into a barbed wire fence. I had no idea this was Amy's home. Would have been fun to have known that in my original timeline. I wonder if Rick still ended up at that party somehow.

There are no other cars in the driveway yet. It is clear the garage can fit at least six vehicles. At the door, I pray this is the right house and not just my twisted memories scratching to the surface. There is no answer. Am I at the right house? Am I that out of practice with land navigation? Maybe it's the house with the loud music blasting nearby. But this is the address I have written down.

A car pulls up with Amy and some of her friends that I kind of recognize. "Jason! You're early. Come help us with this stuff."

They hand me several packs of cheap soda, while they bring in bags of chips. I guess this is going to be a decent sized gathering. We spend some time setting things up. I guess I was really early. One of Amy's friends, I believe her name is Judy, also went to the same middle school.

Judy says, "Dylan was such a jerk, so glad you knocked him down a peg. So, what really happened after you beat him up? I heard you were expelled."

I can see Dylan's bloody face as I smash his skull against the metal basketball stand. It doesn't feel good to remember. I was an adult beating up children, and I don't want to celebrate that. "I got sent to a juvenile detention center, just got released."

"Oh my God," Judy exclaims. "You spent five years in prison because of that? That is a miscarriage of justice. I should know, I'm pre-law."

Amy says, "That's not a thing."

Judy says, "If you're not in med school yet, you're pre-med. Same thing for law students."

They have a minor disagreement as I notice the many scars on my knuckles. There were so many fights, and I never noticed the damage left behind before.

There's a knock at the door. "I'll get it." I want something to distract me.

Before I reach it, Zack bursts in. "Waz up! Let's get this party started!" His silver hair has grown all the way to his shoulders now.

I stand dumb founded with my fists at my waist, not sure how to react. Zack bumps my knuckles. "Good to see you, dude." Then he goes to kiss Judy.

Alex has to duck his head to enter the house. "Long time no see."

I'm still distracted by the display of public affection.

Alex pats me on the shoulder with his huge hand. "Don't mind them. It's honestly a bit much even for me."

"Right. How are you and Katie?" *Shit! I shouldn't have asked that. I don't know if they met in this current timeline. Did I just expose myself?*

Alex says, "We're good. She won't be done with work till later."

Trying not to show my moment of brief panic, I say, "Cool."

Judy hands out drinks. Nothing alcoholic this time, just sodas.

Amy sits me down on the living room couch and says, "You have been gone for five years. Tell us all about it."

I'm starting to think she has an unhealthy obsession with dangerous people. Where are her parents? "Well, I got sentenced to five years for aggravated assault."

Everyone gathers around me in the living room, wanting details. Zack says, "Five years, one for each of those dudes you wrecked."

I cringe a bit at how he says that. "I got into more fights

on the inside. There wasn't much of a choice. I was the youngest, and the older delinquents saw me as a target."

Zack asks, "Did any?" He makes an obscene gesture with his hands, trying to be funny.

Judy smacks him for being vulgar.

I say, "No, but they tried. I sent a kid to the infirmary just for thinking about it." I don't want to talk about my many fights. I permanently messed up a lot of people. Even though I didn't have a choice, looking back on it now doesn't bring a smile to my face.

"Who are you?" says a familiar voice cutting through my poor story.

There at the door stands Rick, his blond afro trimmed short and his skin paler than normal, clearly from lack of sun exposure. "You can't be Jason. Jason Baker is dead." Everyone scoots away from me as Rick gets closer. "Jason Baker died months ago during transport to the state prison, from complications caused by his brain tumor." He looks ready to fight.

I instinctively put up my hands, bracing for combat. "Calm down, Rick. It's kind of a long story."

Rick enters striking range. "I was at the funeral. I watched them bury him. Who are you?"

"I am Jason Baker."

"Prove it!" Rick demands.

How? All the memories I have are contorted from my many jumps through time. The key moments from our childhood were cut out because of my meddling. *What's something that happened before it all changed?*

Rick stands ready to strike the imposter.

I feel ashamed for not having anything. *That's it!* A

moment of shame for which Rick is the only witness. "I once pissed my pants in first grade, and you acted as a shield, blocking others from seeing me as I snuck to the nurse's office for clean pants. That was the moment I knew I could trust you with anything until the day I died."

There is tangible silence in the room, waiting for Rick or me to respond.

I speak first. "I suppose I did die a few times now. There was a government cover up. I escaped the facility, and well…" I make an awkward gesture to myself. "Here I am."

Zack mumbles, "This is better than TV."

Judy gently shushes him but has a clear smile engrossed in the drama.

Rick finally says, "What would the government want with you?"

I say, "There are a few things." I relax my mind to envision an imaginary hand bringing one of the sodas from the fridge to Rick. "Time and space have shifted because of my actions."

Rick takes the floating soda can, absolutely speechless.

I expect panic at my alien ability, only to be met with a memorized Zack saying, "Cool."

My parents accepted everything with open arms, just happy to have me back. Now I guess we will see how these friends will feel. "I'm from a future that no longer exists. The last witness to a war that killed each of you." I point to Alex, Zack, and Rick. "My mind was sent back to 2007. I gave my knowledge of time travel to the government to stop the war." *They don't need to know about Angel.* "Now I fear something worse is on the horizon."

Staring at me with a strange look of infatuation, Amy asks, "What is coming?"

"I don't know, something more devastating."

Amy's father comes into the living room talking to someone on the phone. "Yeah, I'm checking now." He takes the phone away from his ear. "Sorry for the interruption. Apparently, something's happening in Detroit."

Zack objects, "Ah, come on, I was just getting invested."

Amy's father turns on the TV here in the living room, to a live news report in what looks to be a war zone. The reporter says, "It appears Detroit has been hit with some kind of terrorist attack. Emergency crews are working to evacuate people. We do not have a visual of the attackers, only speculation at this time."

There is a high-pitched guttural scream that shakes my brain as the camera pans over a gray figure standing within a circle of something spinning high-speed, destroying everything around the alien being. Cars are hurled into buildings as people are ripped apart.

The reporter says, "The attacker does not appear to be human. Hold on, I'm getting more reports. Yes, we can confirm that we are currently under attack from an alien species. There are attacks currently here in Detroit, the Vatican City in Rome, Mecca in Saudi Arabia, Stalingrad in Russia, and in Wuhan, China."

Amy and her father simultaneously say, "Oh, my God," with an almost tangible fear.

The footage returns to the alien in Detroit. It has destroyed at least three city blocks in its rampage. Strangely, I recognize the gray figure by a large scar on its chest. It is one of the aliens that abducted me from the government compound, yet it seems different. During our last interaction, it was sophisticated and used its power with exact control. Now it swings wildly, throwing everything it can in all directions, closer to a living tornado. Every couple of steps, it stumbles before correcting its crooked path down the street.

The reporter says, "This is indeed a coordinated attack by an alien species."

I say out loud, "Bullshit."

Everyone looks at me.

"I met those things in the government compound where I was held. They helped me escape." I turn from the TV to face everyone. "Why the hell would interstellar aliens launch a ground attack with only five fighters? I know for a fact that they have flying vehicles. Something ain't right about this."

"Says the guy with the same powers as the attacking alien," Alex says inquisitorial.

In hindsight, I probably shouldn't have tapped into The Source in front of everyone. "I don't understand the powers very much right now. They're kind of a recent side effect from my trips through time."

Zack asks, "Won't it make more sense to have time-related powers from that?"

Alex nods. "I was thinking the same thing."

"I did for a bit, but I lost that when the timeline shifted away from the Third World War."

Rick says, "I think World War Three is still happening." He gazes back at the destruction continuing on TV. "Where the heck is the army, or at minimum, the local police?"

Judy says, "Or just someone with a gun to shoot that thing."

"Detroit has strict gun laws. Most people with weapons

obtained them illegally, so I doubt they want to start a fight with a superpowered alien," Rick remarks with his big brain.

I say, "Bullets were ineffective against the one I saw fight, but that one had weapons of its own. This one is disarmed."

As the alien rips through another city block, a helicopter drops off a handful of well-armed soldiers and a larger man in a much more advanced looking suit of body armor. The soldiers flank the alien, opening fire. Only one bullet strikes the alien in the arm where it has a brief moment of recognition before returning to its rampage. Then it is completely obliterated with a large explosion. It looked like a precise artillery strike, but there were too many high buildings around for a hit like that. Artillery takes time to set up, while the alien rampage couldn't have lasted more than forty minutes. Where could the military set off a battery to fire in Detroit? No, an airstrike would be more efficient, but there was no sign that aircraft were scrambled. That soldier in the armor has something new, something far more effective than a grenade launcher under that rifle.

No, no, no. I feel my heart pounding in my ears. It's all going to happen again. I didn't stop a damn thing, only pushed it down the line. There is a small crack in my back as visions of this new future press into reality. Alex's flesh is burned away with fire.

"No, it didn't happen!"

Rick's eyes pop as blood flows freely from his face.

"Not again. Please, not again."

Amy asks, "Jason, are you alright?"

I feel blood drip from my nose as my legs buckle to the call of the Void.

I fear what is to come…

My fight against the Void is pointless as it pulls me back into its intricately simple flow through the universe.

What is this new future?

I stand in a ruined city as the man with red eyes kills God. He turns to me and smiles his perfect white teeth smile. "You're welcome."

"Why?! I did not ask for this!" I gesture to the ruined world around us. "None of us asked for this!"

He steps away from his kill, crushing the severed head in his grasp. "There was no other choice."

In an instant, his fist punches through my chest and sends me back to the void. That doesn't answer any of my questions.

What am I missing? What has become of Angel?

Angel sits in the same room where we last met, his eyes swollen from our fight. The decapitated guard's remains are covered with a tarp. The room is now a crime scene.

The man with red eyes enters the room. "What did you do?" he asks, his voice calm yet stern.

Angel doesn't answer as he stares at the ground with a blank expression.

The man with red eyes grabs Angel by his scalp, lifting him to his feet.

Angel yelps and thrashes against the pain.

"What did you do?"

Angel swings his arms, scratching at the man's face, trying to cause any damage, but only hurts his own hands. He screams at the top of his lungs, "I hate you!"

The man with red eyes gently flicks Angel's nose with his free hand, breaking the bridge with a burst of blood. "What did you *do*?!"

Angel holds his nose, cursing the man in Spanish.

The man squeezes Angel's scalp. "Don't make me ask again."

"Why does it matter? You have everything you wanted. I have nothing. There is nothing left." Angel's eyes tear up. "I am nothing."

I can see his home burning as his family suffers. *This is my fault.*

The man with red eyes says, "Everything matters. Every. Last. Asset." He releases Angel, dropping him to the floor. "Now the enemy could have portal technology and your former friend has become the greatest threat to our species in thousands of years. Pray he is still on this planet, or else we will lose everything again."

Angel spits on the man. "Fuck you, and fuck this planet."

The man with red eyes doesn't wipe away the mucus from his black jacket. "I wish things did not have to be this way, child. I suppose we can replicate your window without you now." He snaps Angel's neck cleanly without any sign of suffering. "It's a shame you became a hindrance to progress."

"Noooooo!" I scream into the void as I try to reach through the unbreaking patterns of time, unable to do a damn thing. "I'm sorry, Angel. I'm so sorry."

I miss the days of simpler times.

"Do you call?"

"Angel?"

I sit at an improvised table in an underground bunker with a pair of twos in my hand.

Luis says, "Any day now, mopey."

"Yeah…right, I call." I toss a crumpled dollar bill into

the pot. There is not much to gamble with in this underground bunker.

Scratching at his unkempt red mustache, Sergeant McIntyre folds. "Damn it. You boys ain't given me a good card all day. Hope we get some grooming supplies in the next drop. I'm starting to feel like a damn hippy."

There is a rumble outside. The bombing of Turkey is still in progress. This was one of the better times in the war.

Angel jokes, "Better be some ass wipe too."

Corporal Humphrey says, "I'll call." His black sunglasses reflect me above his perfect white teeth.

A rage far beyond any comprehension fills me. *That where I know you from!* For the man that orchestrated all this horror sat just in front of me. The bonds of time and space cannot stop this seething hatred, I smash through The Void. Fueled with all the hatred in my heart, I grab Corporal Humphrey by the neck and demand, "What are you?!" He can't escape me now. This is a part of *my* past.

The glasses fall off, revealing his red goat-like eyes. He says still smiling with his perfect white teeth. "I am the necessary evil of humanity."

My grip remains tight. "Who are you?"

"Ya Be Chun."

We stand in a valley of green vegetation and animals I don't fully recognize. They seem very similar to deer but a clear sub spices with red horns. He peels away my grip, saying, "I am the last person to remember what life was like before the sky fell. This is my home, a small village in what is now the North Sea. Ya Be Chun."

A massive wall of water scrapes away everything.

"What happened?"

He points up. "They came." The sky fills with thousands of large disks and millions of people are taken up into the sky from the stone cities around the world. "They wanted intelligent livestock."

People scream in pain as they are skinned and dumped into vats of chemicals. Grotesque medical experiments proceed in mass. Horrors witnessed through his eyes as tall gray men play with human lives for fun in the grossest games. Until his eyes are melted from their sockets. Then what is left of the humans are dumped into the ocean. Where new eyes grow revealing more light than before. A meteor shoots through the atmosphere, impacting a massive iceberg in Greenland and sending flood waters all throughout the world.

"Ya Be Chun."

"Why do you keep saying that?"

"It all happened twelve thousand, eight hundred twenty-five years ago. From the oldest language I can remember, Ya Be Chun. 12 8 25. I am the only one that remembers what truly happened. The other survivors were a handful of small tribes spread across the globe. They remembered the wrath of the heavens in their stories, now myths, while I wandered the Earth and prepared for their next arrival."

He leads a tribe of barbarians into battle against a Roman legion. Mortal wounds only leave behind scars.

"I ruled the largest empire the world had ever seen, only to be defeated and erased by the might of Rome."

"How could an immortal be defeated?"

"Because I didn't change. My people were ruled by strength, mocking new inventions as unimportant. Refusing armor and viewing battle as a chance for personal glory.

I lost everything again. Then I accepted that Rome would build something better than me."

I see he lacked a purpose too. Without death, you saw no meaning in life.

I follow him throughout the world, searching for meaning and fighting battles across the globe without reason. Watching people die. Until we stand in a Japanese city. We see young men in military uniforms with bolt action rifles handing out rations of rice.

Oh no. Where are we?

My eyes lock with a familiar looking ten-year-old Japanese boy as a plane drops something from far above the city.

"Everything changed after the bomb dropped."

Wait, no!

Everything is erased from the heat of the blast. I watch as Corporal Humphrey is flash fried from the heat of the atomic bomb. His skin and muscles ripped from bone, leaving only a skeletal frame full of melted organs, just to rise again. His body reforms with all his scars from history gone.

"That day, everything changed. Humanity has gained too much power. I swore I would never let that happen again. That was the day I took over the world. I forced President Truman and General Secretary Stalin to sign contracts with their blood. After all, who could stop me if a nuclear bomb couldn't."

"Then why do nukes still exist?"

"Because *they* came back."

A massive disc shaped craft lands in the Nevada desert.

"Our weapons of today terrified them. A bunch of primitives with nuclear power and the ability to reach their planets."

"That's why there is still war? You control everything, but you still let these horrors happen?"

"We must continue to grow in the worst way."

"That's horrible. Why couldn't the meteor just kill us all? I don't want this."

"Too bad. This is how it must be."

"What?"

"I said, too bad, life wants nothing more than to survive by any means necessary."

Rage fills my soul and I punched him across the face, knocking out teeth. "That doesn't give you the right to cause such horrors. What about everyone's right to life? Have you fallen so much that you can't see how wrong this is?"

"The catholic church ripped my teeth out centuries ago." He takes out his cracked dentures. "War is not about right or wrong. It is about who is left, and I have been left after every single conflict. I will ensure humanity remains after the next war. We have a predator that won't stop until it is wiped from the galaxy. That is why I do what I do. A utopia is pointless when true evil can take it all away in a flash."

I want to say more but I am pulled back to reality passing through the void, to hit the floor at Amy's house. Everyone is looking at me with concern.

Rick asks, "Are you alright?"

Sitting up, I say, "I think I am."

Then I hear his voice. "We're not done yet, Jason."

Something grabs my very soul, pulling me back into the Void.

"You caused this. Now you're going to see the result."

CHAPTER 19

THE WAR FOR THE STARS

I SEE THROUGH HIS RED EYES but am unable to interact with the world, trapped in a moving prison. He is standing in front of a portal that reflects his pale face. He adjusts his black tie.

"Now the end can begin."

Is he talking to me? I try to say, "What are you going to do?" Yet no sound is produced. I try to move but nothing happens.

With one final straightening of his coat, he says, "None of this would have been possible without you."

Yabechun steps through the portal. On the other side stands a man in a military uniform. His face is swollen with a broken nose. He says, "They are not happy, sir," before limping through the portal.

We stand in a room of five alien beings, each sitting in floating thrones of bright colors. The thrones increase in height, and I assume the highest one is probably of senior authority. I am mesmerized by the colored patterns of the entire room, bright colors of unique blues and greens. The aliens are not a plain gray, but in fact, a strange shade of almost purple. Am I seeing light on the ultraviolet spectrum? I've never seen such bright colors before. Everyone in this room has the same red irises while Yabechun's pupils are oval like goat eyes and theirs are closer to cats.

Yabechun speaks first. "Greetings, oh great powerful ones. I am honored that you have approved our meeting today. It is a shame you had to treat my messenger so poorly." He takes a deep breath. "The extra argon is already off-putting for the lad, not to forget the slight increase of gravity. You did not need to cause him such harm."

Words are not spoken verbally but projected directly into our collected mind. "Foolish primitive. Be thankful we left him alive. How dare you bring such a technology to us." It feels as though that projection came from the lowest being.

"You don't like it? I brought it as a gift." Yabechun exaggerates his disappointment. "That's why I requested this meeting. It takes many human lifetimes for light to reach your planet from ours while your ships can make that trip in a month. Now with what we call Angel's Window, that travel time is instantaneous."

The second lowest alien snaps out, "We know what teleportation is." This voice sounds of a higher pitch. "Clearly you are the one in need of lecturing."

The lowest one says, "What is the point of lecturing a primitive? It is a waste of energy."

They all have similar facial structures with only the slightest of changes to set them apart. There are no wrinkles to determine age, but the highest one has a slight change in ultraviolet color. The second from the top has been staring with a puzzled expression. *Can that one see me?*

"It appears you have brought an additional consciousness to us today."

Oh, shit. What should I do?

"Don't mind him," Yabechun says keeping perfectly composed. "He was instrumental in the creation of this technology. Unfortunately, he could not physically make it."

The same one. "How did he access The Source? Your kind forgot that ability long ago."

Yabechun says, "Yes, many things were lost after your conquest. Yet few have been able to find that inner piece of creation."

"Enough!" the lowest one yells. "We reject this horrible gift, you foolish primitive. The dangers of this technology nearly destroyed all life last time it appeared."

I can feel Yabechun smile. "You mean the war that won you control of the galaxy?"

"How could you possibly know that? It was long before your time."

"Approximately a hundred thousand Earth years before my time. I have learned so much about your history and culture while you delightfully consume our trash television without caring about the art behind it."

The highest creature finally speaks. "The gift must be rejected. Instantaneous travel is a danger that is best forgotten forever. We should have been more thorough in the extinction effort of humans." It turns its focus to the lowest one. "Commander, you may commence the extermination."

"Yes, I do believe it is time to begin a genocide," Yabechun says calmly.

Yellow gas begins to fill the room. *Oh, God, no! Not again, not now.*

Yabechun breathes in the chlorine fumes. "Such a strong aroma, don't you agree?"

The floating thrones crash down to the ground as the aliens begin to cough up blue blood.

"Don't worry with our immortality the symptoms are not fatal. Unfortunately for all of you, I discovered a more permanent solution for our kind."

I am unable to do anything as Yabechun stomps his foot upon the head of one alien, sending its brain matter outward.

"While your people may have created an everlasting life, you never did push it to the limit. Scared of what it would create, you refused to share this gift with your warriors." He tears another's head from its body. "Never felt death on your peripherals." He smashes the skull between his hands. "While I have spent the last thirteen thousand years pushing this body to near death every single day."

One of the aliens tries to crawl away, but Yabechun places his foot on the back of its skull. "Do you feel that? The fear of death as it claws for you." He applies pressure to the alien's head. "That is how every conscious being felt as you toyed with them. Crying for help before…" He crushes the alien's skull across the floor.

He grabs the eldest one by the neck. "You scorched my planet, drowned my people, and raped innocents for your own pleasure. You sacrificed my people to gain everlasting life but never truly tested its limits in your utopia." His grip begins to tighten. "Be thankful that you will finally know the end. You robbed me of that rest, long ago."

The alien screams for help, projecting its mental cries out to its world as bloody tears flow from its red cat-like eyes.

Yabechun's smile reflects back at me through the creature's pupils. "That's not going to work. My invasion began as soon as I walked in here. That's why my messenger had several ship escorts. Now your planet will burn." His grip tightens until the thing's head pops off its body with a sickening sound. "You didn't even share this gift with most of your citizens, and now they will suffer for your sins." Then he crushes the skull with a thundering stomp.

He turns his attention to the military commander now struggling to its feet. "Filthy primitive!" It lobs one of the thrones at us with its telekinetic ability, but without any real force behind it.

I instinctively block only to remember I can't do anything as Yabechun catches the chair with one hand. "All your power, and you never trained your own body's strength." He throws the metal throne back at twice the velocity.

The commander ignites a red blade, slicing the metal throne in half before it can cause damage. "I should have had you killed when we rediscovered your species."

Now the only sound is the light humming of his hyper heated red blade.

"The sad thing is…" Yabechun springs forward, his speed unhindered by the toxic gas.

The commander's swing is slow, feeling the symptoms of chlorine gas exposure.

With one quick movement, Yabechun rips the commander's head from his shoulders. "I had already become a

God by the time you came back." He holds the severed head in his hand.

The commander projects its final thoughts at us. We see all of humanity taken in for experiments over a millennia ago. After successfully figuring out how to replicate everlasting life, all human beings are dumped into the ocean. The experiments are replicated on their own people, creating an immortal ruling class in a far more pleasant environment. Except for one being that is pushed to its physical breaking point a thousand times over, turning this alien being into a monster of immeasurable power. It is dropped onto planets to exterminate all life for the commander's amusement.

I swear the severed alien head smiles, showing the monster's ship headed for Earth.

"You should have pushed the limits yourself, coward." The severed head is crushed in our hands.

I feel my mind drifting back into the void, released from this prison. "Wait!"

"I'll deal with you later, Jason. I have a war to win."

I fall back through the Void, just seeing a glimpse of an alien city being nuked as I return to my own body.

CHAPTER 20

INVASION

T HE TIME HAS ARRIVED, *JOHN.*

Now I go into the fray, leading the greatest army humanity has ever assembled to destroy an alien world. This is my destiny to lead us to conquest in glory. I was born a Kane, born to be a killer, just like my ancestors before me. Now I will use that truth to kill humanity's greatest enemy.

Portals have been deployed across the planet, allowing Earth's Air Forces to unleash a devastating attack across this new globe. One thousand nuclear missiles erupt across the planet, taking out their most populated centers, while chemical weapons are being set off across military bases. The Geneva Convention does not apply to non-humans.

In the aftermath of nuclear destruction, as radiated rains drop black silt across this planet, my job is to lead ground forces to secure vital areas of military interest and begin artillery bombardment. Each of our assault rifles has a small portal attached under the barrel, essentially giving every soldier a portable artillery canon, even though their power sources will not last long. The batteries must be replaced every hour, and if power is cut out, the portals loose connection, becoming useless. Fresh batteries can be placed in before the old ones are taken out. There should be people on the other side of the portals to take the used batteries and give us fresh ones, but there is currently a limited supply until we can capture their industrial sectors where we can make more batteries from elements not found on Earth.

Once the power sources are secured, portal technology can be utilized to its fullest potential for this invasion. Portals set up on jet fighters will allow for near infinite ordnance while people back home can reattach missiles without landing. Or even refuel with a portal set above the tank. Until then, every soldier is still given a standard M5 assault rifle.

If two open portals that are not connected to each other touch, they will instantly deactivate. The solution, each portal has a detachable cover as we cross from our planet to the new world for the invasion.

Our troop transport touches the soil of this new world. Instantly, I feel heavier. Gravity is slightly greater than Earth but not enough to cause serious health issues, so says military intelligence. With my strength enhancements, the weight increase feels close to nothing, maybe an extra pound of gear. The plants do produce oxygen from carbon monoxide, same as Earth. They just produce an additional amount of argon, again not too harmful, just tastes funny. At least that's what the briefing said. Everyone has on full hazmat gear to protect them from the radioactive dust now contaminating this planet's air. The yellow star is blocked out by the clouds dropping black rain on obliterated cities where only the frames of massive super structures stand ready to crumble.

So this is what it looks like when all rules of war are

thrown out. It's kind of beautiful in a fucked-up way. In all my deployments to the Middle East, hardly anything ever got done as we fought guerrilla militants in civilian clothing. Rules were in place to stop us from doing the job we were sent to do. Now we can kill with impunity.

My objective is to take a military base, claiming their space craft for our own. Once the crafts are secured, they will be outfitted with military grade weaponry to secure air dominance. This is their home world, and there are many planets under their control. Time is limited before their off-world armada launches a counter offensive. The base has already been hit with a missile of Sarin gas, bringing every nearby enemy to their knees. I deploy my troops to finish off the survivors before they can recover.

We move quickly, not giving our enemy time to bounce back. We're executing every gray being with a shot to the head. It is strange that none of them have the same uniform jumpsuit. What kind of military allows for such a failure of discipline? I have witnessed their telekinetic abilities. One trained soldier took out an entire platoon and a helicopter. The gas was meant to bring them down to our level and keep them from using that unnatural ability, but most died from the gas exposure. It's kind of pathetic that of the hundred flying saucers in this shipyard, not one is outfitted with weapons. Hell, none of these alien soldiers have any kind of weaponry on them, not like the one on Earth that had those flying red blades that could cut through steel. Honestly, I was hoping to take one of those swords for myself, spoils of war.

I don't think this is a military base. I think this is just a parking lot for spacecraft. These Xeons have given intergalactic travel to their civilians! That much power at an individual level is absolutely insane. No wonder they abducted humans for fun. That's impossible to police. I know for a fact that humans would do the exact same thing if given the chance. That's why it's not safe to hitchhike anymore.

The area is quickly secured and alien bodies are piled up to be burned while portals are set up for the engineers to do their work. Our standard infantry takes up positions to hold this location while I take my elite team to the next target.

This barely feels like a real fight. I wonder if Igor, James, and Jin are facing any real resistance. Hercules is probably having more fun than any of us.

One of the infantry soldiers jumps on an alien corpse, smashing its brains outward. "Take that, filthy Xeno." He kicks the brain matter into a burn pit. "That's for Detroit." The name tag on his uniform says Melvin. I don't interrupt, wanting the grunts to use their hate.

Helicopters are brought through a portal to take my troops to the next point of interest—a refinery of their precious fuel for these crafts. We will work up the supply line until humans control every aspect of high-speed space travel. According to Yabechun's plan, with control of both portal technology and interplanetary travel that takes less than a lifetime to reach another solar system, "We will gain control of the entire galaxy before the name of Kane dies out."

I will do my job for the glory of humanity.

CHAPTER 21

FAMILY

"**J**ASON? CAN YOU HEAR ME?" A calm voice speaks as a hand forces my eye open to a bright light.

I immediately react, smacking her hand as I roll away, right off a stretcher and onto the hard tile floor. I keep moving, trying to figure out my surroundings and then bracing myself against a wall, ready for a fight. I find myself in a white room with a woman in light blue scrubs standing by the stretcher I just fell out of.

Holding her hands up with a flashlight in one hand, she says, "Jason, please calm down."

I relax just a little. "Sorry, old habits." But I stay in the corner, keeping my eye on a potential exit. "Where am I?"

"Yuma Regional Hospital," she says, looking at me like a potential threat. "Please sit back down. You may have a concussion."

"I wouldn't doubt it, but I'm afraid I can't do that." I'm still in my street clothes, probably just got here. My name has already been placed in the computers, so it won't be long before government agents come for me.

Fearing this nurse is about to yell for security, I extend my consciousness and force her mouth shut. When she is unable to make a sound and struggles against the invisible hands holding her jaw tight, the look of fear in her eyes brings me to a level of guilt I forgot I had.

I rush to the door. "I'm sorry about that. Listen, when some people come asking about me, tell them you haven't gotten a chance to see me yet. Your life will be much easier."

I release her, and she drops to her knees gasping for breath. That was too rough. I still need to practice this power. I quickly walk out the nearest door labeled exit only to end up in the Emergency Department Lobby where everyone from Amy's house is watching the news. The only news story is the alien attack across the globe. Vatican City is still under siege. They are showing footage of the unstable alien tearing apart the ancient structures.

Rick sees me first. "Dude, are you alright?"

"Yeah, all good. Let's go." Quickly maneuvering around the rows of chairs to my escape.

Alarms blare as someone announces through the intercom system, "Code Silver. Armed patient, white male in black shirt. I repeat, Code Silver, armed patient, white male in black shirt."

Everyone in the lobby looks at me, realizing I fit the exact description.

A security guard yells, "Freeze, dirtbag!" pointing a revolver at me.

I don't move. I need to be gentler this time. Keep my mind calm. Just need to deescalate this situation. Remember the water, picture your own hands interacting with the gun.

He didn't cock the hammer. I pop out the cylinder containing the bullets and eject them at the guard. The alarm stops as the brass bounces off the tile floor. The guard curses, about to reload.

I say, "You're not paid enough for this. Just let it go." Then I make the speed loaders drop all his extra rounds with a simple twist.

With that, I walk right out the front doors, not stopping until Rick catches me halfway through the parking lot. "Where are you going, man?"

"I don't know, and it's best if you don't know either."

"What the hell are you talking about?!" Rick exclaims. "We were freaking out after you passed out. What the hell happened to you?"

I turn back to see all my friends. There is a life I wish we all could have had. Growing old, laughing at dumb jokes together. "I have to face the reality I've created. The war has already begun, and I have to end it. Promise me you'll stay out of this fight."

Rick is too confused to answer.

I grab him by his shoulders, extending my new power and lifting him slightly in the air. "Don't join this war. Find your own path in this life." I release him, letting him drop back down. "My destiny has a bitter end."

Zack says, "Too bad. We're coming too."

"No!" I protest.

Zack now stands between Rick and I, a steady hand on both our shoulders. "I have regretted not helping you fight Dylan. We should have had your back during that fight because that's what friends do. So too bad, you're not going at this alone."

Rick says, "I wanted to help you back then, but I was too much of a coward. I blamed myself for you dying in prison. Now you're here, and I'm not going back down just because you say so."

"You guys don't understand the danger. Real monsters you can't possibly understand are going to be unleashed," I say while trying to back away, only to bump into Alex who somehow got behind me.

Alex says, "Then help us understand. I've been onboard for whatever happens next after you moved a soda can with your mind. Now you disarm a gun without touching it."

Even Amy chimes in. "This sounds way more interesting than working for my dad. I'm all in."

Her father shrugs, "Stock meetings put anyone to sleep."

I consider using my power to push them away and then running until I hear an RV honk its horn twice and remember we're standing in the middle of a hospital parking lot. Expecting to hear the driver cuss at us, I'm surprised by Mr. Shimizu.

He leans out the window and says, "I knew you would be here."

In that moment I can see it, a future past the pain. I don't have to go at it alone anymore. "Alright, but understand this. There will be no going back. I am a legally declared dead delinquent on the run from the United States government."

All my friends give me a nod of understanding. Amy has a smile that worries me just a bit. She's way too excited for this. Half of us pile into Mr. Shimizu's RV and half get into Amy's father's car. The plan is to meet at my place, to get ready to live off the grid for a while.

Arriving home, I'm caught off guard by seeing my whole family there all at once. They are gathered around the TV, watching footage of the alien attack. The story has pivoted to a counter offensive with an invasion of the alien home world, followed up by recruitment commercials to defend our world from foreign invaders. They even had commercials ready, so this was definitely all planned out months ago, if not years in advance.

"Dad, prepare the camping gear. We need to disappear for a while. Pete, help Dad. We need to move fast." I am Lieutenant Baker again.

Everyone tries to ask questions, but I stop them, bringing out the voice of my old drill Sergeant. "Shut it! Men will be coming for me, and they will gladly end all of our lives." I see fear in my mother's eyes. "I will get us out of here. Gather all the food in this house that can last a while. We leave in twenty."

They stare back at me, frozen in confusion.

"Move! Move! Move!" I clap my hands, sending everyone off in different directions.

I steal an old pair of my brother's hiking boots as well as some clothing. I was going to get hand-me-downs anyway, in my original timeline. Then I take the alien cylinder I got back in the desert, thinking if it can wound the man with red eyes, then it can end him once and for all.

A war with another planet has begun, the police are probably after me, the man with red eyes is going to "deal with me," and there is a monster more powerful than him heading to the planet. How the hell am I going to deal with all that? My panic subsides ever so slightly as I see all my friends, and Amy's father for some reason, waiting for me outside my home. At least with my family behind me, ready for an apocalypse, I know I can face the end of the world.

CHAPTER 22

THE BACK LINES

"**G**ENERAL WILLIAM KANE." A COLONEL radios me from the Alien world. "We have captured the refineries."

"Thank you," I say, writing down everything I have gathered before issuing my next order. "Hold until engineers arrive with the army, then advance into the capitols, clear of all hostiles."

He says, "Understood, sir," then hangs up.

The army better not keep my marines waiting. This war will be won based on our speed. Destroy the enemy, capture their spacecraft, and take control of their fuel source. My marines lead the charge against the enemy while the army holds our new territory and prepares for the counterattack. It is only a matter of time before their armadas arrive. Our Air Force will have to fight them off with untested pilots in retrofitted alien craft.

It is amazing that I am coordinating a war light years away, all thanks to these portals. That being said, I would rather be there with my men, charging into the fray at their side. I don't know if that is my inner marine or my family curse wanting blood. It doesn't matter. I'm too old to be on the front lines anymore. I'll just have to guide this current generation from the 32nd Street Navy station in San Diego. Still, I like to stay armed, so I've got my grandfather's Colt .45 Peacemaker on my hip. This gun saved me in 'Nam when my M16 jammed. I don't feel comfortable in war without it.

My watch rings. "Time to report to the big boss."

I walk through a series of portals from our command center in DC to a base I don't recognize, but based on the climate, I would guess the Mojave desert. Then a final portal ends up bringing me to a well-lit, climate-controlled library. Analyzing my environment, I almost walk into several soldiers pushing a stack of boxes on a cart. They apologize for almost running into me before continuing.

Almost all the shelves of this library have been cleared as people work to box up and categorize everything. Texts of old English cover the shelves, yet the metal shelving and protective glass is clearly modern. *Where am I?*

"What do you have to report to the general?" asks the familiar tone of Yabechun as he sits in an office chair, reading from a book I believe to be written in Latin.

"One thousand two hundred fifty-five nuclear bombs have been detonated on the alien world. The planet is entering nuclear winter. Radiation has contaminated all the native life. We have captured twenty thousand spacecraft and now control almost all their fuel refineries."

He closes his book, turning his red eyes to me. "Casualties?"

"Few and far between. The use of gas and the radioactive

fallout has neutralized the alien's ability to use their telekinesis and without that, they are far too weak to oppose us physically."

He smiles. "Excellent. I knew their home world would be vulnerable. Arrogance is such a powerful weakness. Their counterattack is estimated to be a week away. Cleanse the planet and prepare defensives. The air forces of our world will have to take it from here. Then while they are engaged in the void of space, you will destroy their war worlds."

I say, "Understood, sir. Will you be joining on the front?" His power is equal to a living sixty megaton bomb. I once saw him kill a rebel camp of a hundred men in less than a minute using nothing but his own hands. With him, victory is all but guaranteed.

"No, I need to be here."

"What! Why?"

He stands and turns to walk away, gesturing for me to follow. "Our enemy is releasing its greatest weapon. As I was a failed experiment, they are sending a successful one to kill all life on this planet. The meteor didn't work last time, life endured. Even our nukes only leave temporary scares. This coming monster will kill every single conscious being on our planet one by one."

"Sir, we found it." A private shouts as she rushes around the boxing of religious looking artifacts.

"Thank you, Shella." He then proceeds to follow her. "It will land here, where I will face it alone."

"Where is *here*?" I ask, afraid I already know the answer.

Shella leads us to a wooden box bound in leather.

Yabechun crushes the old metal lock with one hand

before gently opening the case. "Are you a religious man, Will?"

That's a tough one. I run my thumb across my grandfather's pistol, feeling the engraved silver cross. "I believe I am. I was baptized, as were all my children. I may not go to church as much as I did when I was younger. I believe the last prayer I ever spoke was before my sister's trial," I answer as truthfully as I can.

He takes out an even smaller box not much larger than a deck of cards. "Then you don't listen to the Pope for how to live your life?"

"No, I live by what the military tells me."

He smiles, showing me his perfect teeth before taking out his dentures. "We are in the archives of Vatican City, the last bastion of Rome." He opens the box, revealing thirty-two teeth complete with roots intact. "It has been so long since these were stolen from me." He picks them up, inspecting them as if they were a great treasure. "Around us is humanity's true history archived by what was the most powerful corporation on the planet. Now all this knowledge is mine." He shoves one of the molars into his gums, causing blood to ooze out before it pulls back in, sealing the tooth in place.

I immediately say, "This is going to lead to a war against the US. We need to keep everyone united to bring up recruitment numbers. This will only paint us as opportunist satanic worshipers."

"You never were very good at scheming, William." He places the next tooth in his mouth. "Your father shouldn't have taught you to be better, Jack knew how to out think his enemies. You are too reliant on brute force. As of right now, the United Nations is providing humanitarian aid to the victims of the alien attack while we secure everything of value before they attack again."

All around us, soldiers move renaissance paintings and sculptures through the back to the Mojave portals.

"We will be able to pay for the cost of this war. I may control the value of money these days, but merely printing it to pay everyone will lead to inflation. Value is needed to back it, and we are surrounded by humanity's greatest treasures." He lets out a genuine laugh for the first time in front of me. "I can't tell you how long I've wanted to get in these caves. After Rome destroyed my empire, after the Church captured me and spent years torturing me. Little did we know every injury only added to my strength. Now it is all mine! Finally…"

He composes himself, straightening out his suit. After he clears his throat, he says, "Return to the war. I will remain here to face the next enemy."

"Understood, sir." Then I leave the way I came.

He finally let his composed nature slip. I always had a feeling he was crazy—everyone is a little. After centuries of life, it is almost to be expected.

The thought takes me back to the night I fought the tiger in the dark. As it clawed at my face and bit into my arm, I split its guts with my knife. Then I stabbed it over and over again. When it was over, I just sat there alone in the jungle, laughing like a maniac, only to be reminded of the war around me by erupting gunfire. I was only armed with a knife and my grandfather's pistol. That was easily one of the most fun nights of my life.

One has to let go of sanity to survive war. Yabechun must have centuries ago to be able to fight the way he does. I suppose that's what happened to Barry. Austin will face it soon. I wonder how John is dealing with it.

CHAPTER 23

GENOCIDE

M Y NAME IS JONATHAN KANE, but to these Xeons, I am the reckoning incarnate. Survivors of the bombing were rounded up during the ground invasion. They are unable to project their unspoken words into my mind, for every soldier's helmet has a protective layer of lead. Then with one precision artillery strike, they are removed from existence. This process is repeated over and over across this planet by each human military involved in the invasion. They did not deserve this paradise. If they had, they would have made a greater effort to protect it. One day when the radioactive smoke clears, we shall rebuild this planet in our image as God intended.

There is no mercy to be had for these creatures as we send their radiation burned bodies to oblivion. The mission will be completed before our new ship armada is fully operational. We know the enemy took over the galaxy millennia ago, but in the past three generations of their species, they have grown lazy. The ease of their extermination stands as proof.

This planet had no military defense to speak of, the fools. According to intelligence, their warriors are roughly fifty thousand light years away, on a planet with about three times earth's gravity. That must make them quite strong, unlike these string beans. They've deployed ships, but even with interstellar travel, it will take them a week to reach us.

With the final pockets of resistance being cleared, I return with my platoon to the staging area—a massive field of pristine granite covered in spacecraft being retrofitted with nuclear ballistic missiles as well as mounted machine guns. It's the first time since the cold war ended that nuclear weapons are being manufactured in mass. I'm proud that I get to see it all used on a proper enemy.

My men go through a portal back to Earth for decontamination and resupply before our next mission. I'm fairly certain all-natural life on this planet has been eliminated. If not, the current freeze of the nuclear winter should finish the job relatively soon. Without proper seasons, there is no hope for plant life to recover.

Before I leave, I take another look at the burned planet. This is a site I never thought I would see. I have the best job in the world and only wish the gear was more comfortable. Taking off my helmet to scratch my irritated scalp under my radiation protected suit, I hear screams of pain as someone begs for mercy.

There is no threat behind this scream. Even without it being vocalized, I can tell its point of origin. What could be happening that a telekinetic voice can pierce through the radioactive fallout. I follow it past our barricades to a ditch hidden from sight. Now I hear the audible sounds of grunting mixed with laughter. My rifle ready, I peek down to see three human soldiers enjoying the spoils of war as the larger of the men is forcing himself upon one of the aliens with his far larger frame. I believe it to be one of the females of the Xeno species, based on its slender features and genitals. It begs them for mercy. As none of them are wearing helmets, I know they can hear her.

With my rifle still ready to fire, I shout, "What the hell are you doing?"

Now in a panic, the three men rush to cover themselves. Unsure of what to do. Knowing I have the drop on them. If I wanted too, I could kill them all.

"What the hell are you morons thinking?"

One looks away while the other two exchange a look. The one with his pants currently down says jokingly, "Trying out the local cuisine, sir."

In no mood for jokes, I march right up to him and plant my boot square in his gut, knocking him on his ass. He heaves with pain, though I barely put any weight behind that. If I wanted to, I could have kicked through him.

"This planet has been coated in nuclear dust! And you have penetrated an alien species with your seed! What is your major malfunction? I should kill all of you now before a new form of AIDs spreads through the human race."

One of the privates says, "Unlikely. This species eliminated all diseases centuries ago." He tries to adjust oversized glasses under his gas mask.

I shove the butt of my gun into his stomach, sending him to the ground. Then I point my rifle at the third, expecting him to say something.

His hands shoot up in surrender. With fresh fear, he confesses, "I hadn't had a turn yet."

I pick up the one with his pants down, my hand completely covering his skull. Reading his name tag, I say, "Melvin, you worthless pile of meat. Pray to your god that you haven't caught anything, or I will have your bodies burned on this planet with the rest of the Xenos. Is this the only one you found?"

Melvin can't be more than eighteen. My hand squeezing his head, he blurts out, "It is!" Then I drop him, and he quickly pulls up his pants.

The alien female whispers in my mind, "Thank you." Fighting against the effects of radiation sickness.

With a burst of gunfire, I end its life. "I will not allow contamination," I say, dropping a phosphorus grenade to burn the remains before forcibly escorting the fools back to post.

I send the men into the medical tent for quarantine before they can cross back over to Earth, informing the medical staff of their actions, not sparing any detail. Then I find their commanding officer. "I want every single one of your men to be quarantined and replaced with another company until I know for certain there have been no viral contaminations. Am I understood, Captain Miles?"

The far smaller man cowers beneath my massive, armored frame. "I understand, Major Kane. It will be done." Then he rushes off, barking orders to his Army company.

The mechanics all look confused, whispering questions to one another. I address them, "You don't have time to worry about them. We need these spacecraft to be combat ready in three hours. Get back to work!" They get back to the installations as I continue to shout. "If you're done, help out another team. The Chinese have already deployed. Are you going to let the Russian and Indian militaries beat you too?"

I return to Earth with my current task completed. After the standard quarantine procedure to remove all radioactive dust, I find a phone call from Yabechun is waiting for me. "Hello, sir."

"Status report?"

I can picture him sitting comfortably in what was the pope's holy throne, probably reading a book written by a monk's firsthand account of the Roman Empire during the transfer from BC to AD.

"All my sections have been cleared of Xeno populations."

"Good. We are at a ninety-five percent population elimination of our enemy. Has there been much resistance?"

"Few and far between. The dust from the nuclear fallout has completely prevented them from using their telekinetic abilities."

He lets out a slight chuckle of satisfaction at that. "They're bodies are weak. Eliminating all disease, illnesses, and strife on their planet was a foolish mistake. Any disruption to their untested immune system completely cripples them. That's why it took us decades to create a rabies strain that caused their powers to flux continually. Have you encountered any rabid aliens?"

"One, but it was easily eliminated with an artillery strike. The others must have been wiped out during the initial bombing."

"Possibly, but not guaranteed. Now I need you to prepare for the counterattack. Their warriors will not fall victim to the nuclear dust as easily. In about five hours, the Chinese fleet will engage with the enemy's armada. They will need US support. Igor says the Russians are almost ready for deployment, but I have learned to take their technological strides with a grain of salt. There is still a chance that the enemy will land a ground force to retake their planet. Use the last five percent of the population as bait. Then wipe them all from existence."

Looking at my robotic hand. "Will they be as strong as the one I fought on Earth?"

"They will."

"Then I look forward to the challenge," I reply, been unable to stop smiling since this operation began.

He says, "We both are."

I imagine Yabechun as he hangs up the phone. His grip crushing the armrest of his new throne as he feels real excitement for the first time in centuries.

CHAPTER 24

WITHIN THE VOID

I CAN SEE IT ALL NOW. A planet cleared of all life as new rulers stake their claim. The drums of war thunder across the stars as a great empire's warriors rushes to maintain control against a hungry rising power. Hundreds of thousands of ships have been sent to defend their home world, hoping beyond hope they are not too late. They can hear the voices being silenced the same as I.

The armada is met by a wall of nuclear bombs erupting across the void of space, each explosion turning into expanding suns that consume ships at the speed of light. With diminished numbers, the two powers clash in the void in between planets. They unleash weapons of absolute destruction upon one another, for only one can remain to control the galaxy.

A smaller envoy of ships lands to see their home world burned to ash. Cries of pain echo, turning into a need for revenge. Blades extend as they charge the evil that destroyed their once beautiful land, only to be obliterated by humanity's great weapons. Swords that can cut through steel are useless against artillery fired from far away.

I stand alone in a demolished city, surrounded by corpses of a nearly extinct alien race.

The one survivor sees me through the void. "Why?"

"I'm sorry. War is fought by foolish youths for old men that hate people they have never met."

A large, armored figure stands above the wounded creature. The alien tries to ignite its blade, but the armored soldier catches the alien's arm, crushing its bone with a metal hand. The alien drops its weapon before its skull is stomped in.

The armored man picks up the hilt, extending the red blade and reducing it back to a hilt, clearly amused by his trophy.

"I hope it was worth it, John."

He doesn't hear me. His mind is closed from the truth.

There is a familiar voice whispering to the void, "I'm not ready."

Across the planet, a human outpost has been laid to waste. Soldiers cut to pieces by scorching blades. Portals flickering off as their power runs out just as the last alien reaches Earth to fill their desire for retribution of their lost home world.

The only voice for miles says, "Please...I'm not done yet."

Upon a pile of dismembered parts lies a third of the man I knew as Hercules in another time. With his one remaining arm, he holds his guts into his body. His lower half lays several feet away. His protective helmet is shattered, and he breathes the poisoned air of this planet. With death clutching hold, he can clearly see. "God?"

"No, I'm a friend from another life." I sit down next to him, holding onto his spirit as it fades from this life.

He yells in defiance, "You don't understand. I'm not done!"

"It's okay, my friend."

"No! You don't understand." He pleads, "There so much I didn't get to do. I never had a girlfriend. I've never known love. I was promised a life. *He* promised me a life." Tears pour down his face. "He *promised* me."

"None of us truly get what we want."

His memories lay bare before me. A childhood in an orphanage full of abuse and neglect. Before men in black suits take him away for experimentations with the promise of heroism. As his body is broken, then rebuilt. He only remembers pain.

Then I see a moment of laughter. Him and another boy named James cover the toilet paper in an officer's bathroom with chili powder while Igor does the same to the toothbrushes. There is laughter as they are chased by the officers.

I share the memory of him beating me during the grappling tournament at boot camp.

"Jason?" Seeing me for who I was to him in the original timeline, he smiles as he passes from this life.

In the once great holy city, I find the man with red eyes sitting in the pope's chair with his feet resting on the pope's hat, as he drinks a clear glass of bleach. He's reading a stone tablet carved over five thousand years ago. The great hall has been stripped barren and all sculptures dragged away. The only accompanying sound is the faint squeaking of a wheel from a cart pulling away a pile of stone tablets to a portal far out of sight.

I ask, "Are you satisfied?"

He does not look up from the tablet. "Listen here, boy. Just because you can see through the void, that doesn't make you special. You are not the first and you most definitely are not the last."

"I wouldn't be satisfied either. You do know that the Holy Roman empire isn't the actual successor to Rome, right?"

Annoyed by my presence, he says, "Do not speak to me about history. I lived it. You only read the lies left behind."

How dare he treat this with such neglect, after all the pain he's caused me. Anger fills me and my connection to the Source flickers, I move to meet his gaze. "You know how this ends, right?"

He laughs, taking his feet down.

I'm suddenly feeling awkward even in this state between understandings. Yet my anger does not waver.

He stands, his eyes seeing me clearly. "It ends when I say it ends. Not one second sooner." His smile disappears. "I have killed more people in my lifetime than you will ever know. If I wanted to, I could kill every last person on this planet with my bare hands. You breathe now because there are bigger things at stake than an angry child that thinks he's special. Now tell me, with all your power, have you looked inward at your own great failures?" He steps toward me, as I suddenly feel vulnerable through my projection. "You're still weighed down by the lives you took, unable to accept the horrors you committed. I have accepted the weight of every life I have taken and will snuff out."

Feeling small, I search for a comeback. "The war you started now flows back to Earth and you're here reading alone."

"Humanity is entrusted in its own victory. While this"—he holds up the tablet of scribbles I can't read—"is the only thing left behind by one of the few people I ever loved. Her last words were stolen from me by this corporation a thousand years ago. Now they have finally found their way back to me."

I suddenly feel a need to apologize, but instead I remain silent.

He turns his back, returning to his stolen throne. "Leave me, child. The final battle of this war will be here soon enough."

Then I am back in the desert, but not the desert I call home. Instead, I am on the other side of the world. A man my age eats a home cooked meal with his parents as they talk about the war. His mother is worried while his father remains stoic. He cracks jokes to bring levity about his day at school.

Who is this person, and why am I seeing this?

I watch as he shares his first kiss with his high school sweetheart just before he is shipped out, promising her they will marry when he returns.

He fires his QBZ from a window, at American soldiers in a war-torn city.

I know this skyline. The skyscrapers with every window broken. Tan buildings with intricate carvings. Ancient mosques covered in bullet holes. This is Baghdad.

There is a commotion behind him in the hallway. He rushes to the door, hoping to not be overrun. He sees three soldiers bunched up by the stairs. Without time to properly aim, he fires from the hip only to be struck in the chest with three bullets. The impact knocks him down and he clutches to life. Without air in his lungs, he cries for his mother. His life ends as his killer runs past yelling, "Meatball, get back here!"

This was my first kill. He had a life, same as me. I stole that from him because I had a better placed shot. It was nothing but luck. "I'm sorry."

I don't want to see this, yet my eyes remain fixed on it.

The man passes through the void and says, "You can't change what you did. You better make it worth something."

I see the lives of every person I killed in the bayonet battle of Baghdad. Each one is so similar it feels like looking in a mirror as I kill myself over and over again. Blood drips from my old body as I bleed to death. Jason falls, entering the void for the first time. I call out to myself, yet nothing is heard as I could not yet process what I was seeing. Then the defibrillator prevents an early death.

There is a great flash of light as I stand alone in what was a city of blown down buildings shrouded in dark clouds. This is Kunduz after the bomb sent me back. This is my original timeline. I walk the streets as black rain falls, cooling sand that superheated into glass. I find the remains of my platoon, shadows burned into the ground. I wonder if they got sent through time as I was. There are fresh tire tracks. Austin Kane stole my Humvee and is now driving away, his body half burned as he fights to get out of the fallout zone. Lucky bastard, it's a damn miracle that the vehicle can still drive. It must have additional lead layers to protect the engine from the electromagnetic pulse. Maybe *not* naming my car was lucky after all.

All time is linear as I follow how life carries on. The war ends, and everyone returns home. The global population has been reduced by a fourth as an armistice is decided with no clear victors. Industries shift to new forms of technology with greater efficiency while world governments have a harder time keeping alien abductions under wraps as there is a spike in activity. With portal technology as yet undiscovered, the aliens do as they please unimpeded.

The man with red eyes continues his rule from the shadows, doing everything possible to rebuild the world. Piles of paperwork and endless meetings. Ordering the deaths of thousands who hold grudges from the war. He's doomed himself to this life of high stakes monotony. He looks at me uncaring as he continues to fill out paperwork. I am one of billions of souls haunting him. I almost pity this person.

Finally, I see what has become of my family. My body was vaporized, but a memorial is held for every Yuma resident that lost a loved one in the war. Alphabetically, my name is second from the top. Jason C. Baker, in brass print on a block of granite in an old cemetery. My high school principal gives a speech about the loss of youth. Even in my death, he is boring. It does not stop my mother from crying. Then flowers are placed by every person who lost someone. Austin Kane limps up to the grave memorial half his face horribly scarred. He doesn't say a word, he places a quarter on my name. A silent way of saying he was there when I died, before vanishing into the crowd.

Time continues to move. My sister Anna met an EMT while working as a nurse. They marry and have three kids, naming their only boy after me. My brother Pete remains a bachelor until a one-night stand gives him a daughter. He never marries but stays in his daughter's life.

At a family Christmas fifteen years after the war, my family fusses over a camera, trying to get a family picture with everyone in it. My nephew keeps making bunny ears over his sister's head. His mother keeps slapping his hand away, saying, "Be nice." My father argues with my brother on how to get the camera timer to start. Then it starts beeping. My brother rushes back to stand on the end next to his daughter. As the flash of the camera ignites, I stand behind my nephew smiling, with tears in my eyes. I see the shadow of myself left behind in the picture. For one moment I am a part of this life one last time.

Now I return to the world that needs me. Air enters my lungs for what feels like the first time. Seeing the faces of my friends and family looking at me, I say, "I know where this will end."

CHAPTER 25

COUNTERATTACK

"**D**O YOU WANT TO KNOW the best part of not being on the front line?" I ask my young assistant as he hands me a fresh cup of coffee.

The fresh-faced private asks, "Is it the coffee, General Kane?" The kid is trying to seem smart.

"No, no, no. You're thinking too small." I gesture to the officer's quarters of 32nd Street Naval Base in San Diego. "It's getting to sleep in a real bed without bugs in your boots. It's the air-conditioning. It's warm food and real toilet paper. It's all the little things."

He says, "And the coffee's good too, sir."

"Yes, now get back to work. We have a war to finish."

The kid rushes off, taking paperwork to another officer while I continue to look at the map of the alien home world.

"Almost done." It is a nice relief to be fighting an enemy where there are no innocents after the last forty years' worth of wars between countries. Each fight descended into long quagmires, because killing civilians is a violation of the Geneva Conventions. This time I am able to unleash the full destructive power the United States has been stockpiling for the past sixty years. This is truly a glorious moment, and I'm glad I skipped retirement for this.

Admiral Cecil Henry walks in, switching from sunglasses to his prescription spectacles. "Did I miss the coffee order, Will?"

I say, "Yes, but the runner ain't far."

"Probably better off just taking a nap. Not that there would be much sleep with all the aircraft taking off and landing." Cecil rubs his eyes, making them even more red. "Feels like this war has been one non-stop squash match. In less than five days, we have completely decimated our adversary. Tell me, Will, do you think we'll look back at this moment in history the same way we see the Nazis after World War Two?"

I catch myself scratching my cheek scar again. "I'm sure there will be some hippies that feel that way. But that is not for us to worry about, not while there is a job to be done. So stay awake. Once the alien home world is ours, we will be moving onto the next planet. China has already engaged their armada. How long until our forces are airborne?"

"Current estimation"— Cecil does math in his head as he looks through his notes—"should be taking off now." He reviews the math again before nodding. "Yeah, they should be taking off."

An intelligence officer comes in with the latest reports. "Sir, American forces have deployed spacecraft."

Cecil does some more math. "We should be engaging the enemy in fifty minutes."

"We're cutting it awfully close." I feel the need to ask, "Were you a math major in college?"

Cecil says, "Bachelor of Science from the US Navy Academy. Did you go to college?"

"Nah, got kicked out of art school for eating crayons."

Cecil looks shocked by that. "Really?"

"Christ, Cecil. It's a joke. I joined the marines at seventeen. I'm a grunt at heart." I twirl my grandfather's Colt .45 Peacemaker to show off my skills. "This little guy has seen more action than you will ever know." I holster the pistol as an Intel officer brings another report. "My grandfather fought with it in two world wars." I always feel a need to share this gun's incredible history.

In a panic, the officer spurts out, "Sir, we've lost contact with the third battalion."

"Well, shit. Did they deploy spacecraft?" I feel nervous for the first time in this war.

The officer looks worried. "Current estimates say that only a third of their ships made it off world. No idea where the rest are."

"Looks like the enemy has some fight in them after all." Everyone is just standing around, so I yell, "What are you waiting for? Get reinforcements there now!"

The constant sound of jets taking off in the bay is cut short as fire erupts from one of the aircraft carriers. The large ship splits in two and half lifts in the air.

Pushing Admiral Cecil to the exit, I start barking orders. "Evacuate! Hostiles have breached the portals. Everyone out!" Checking that my Colt .45 has all six chambers loaded, "Someone get me the PA!" I need to make an announcement to the reserved troops still stationed here.

Fifty thousand tons of steel rise above the city of San Diego, the metal bending to its own weight. The horror of what is about to happen dawns on me. "We should have evacuated the city for this operation."

Would more portals in between us and the alien home world be safer?

"General Kane! I have the base PA here," yells a private with a desk phone.

This is no time to be asking what-ifs. Now is the time for action. I take the phone. "Attention! This is General William Kane. The enemy has breached the portals. Have all artillery portals ready to repel the attack. We are not losing any ground to these freaks." I look at Cecil. "We are going to need air support."

Cecil looks concerned. "Our aircraft don't stand a chance in a fair fight against theirs."

"Doesn't matter. We need something in the air to provide support or at least a distraction." If enemy spacecraft exit the atmosphere, satellites will be taken out. Then it's only a matter of time before they reach the asteroid belt and begin bombarding the planet. Yabechun left one ship out there as a contingency, but that's a lot of space to cover alone.

The shadow of the fractured aircraft carrier casts its long shadow across the city as fires spread to the shore. Outside the command center, troops rush from being woken up to take up arms as attack helicopters take off, firing missiles at the floating ship. Explosions pierce the ship's hull just as it drops onto the city of over a million people, crushing buildings as if they were made out of paper. Its momentum does not simply stop with a thud. Instead, it rolls over everything in its path, breaking apart into metal chunks and ripping through the inhabitants of the beautiful city. Then fires engulf what is left. The attack helicopters are taken out by speeding red disks before they can return fire.

Why didn't they aim for the base?

My assistant mutters, "My God," at seeing real destruction for the first time.

I see that he has a pouch for binoculars and take them without asking. Focusing on the portals the Aliens came through, I say, "The portals have been destroyed. This is a ground assault of one force."

Cecil asks, "What does that mean?"

"It means they don't have any reinforcements. Cancel the evacuation!" I begin directing teams of marines to repel the Xeno incursion. While noncombatants are sent though our base portal to Washington.

Then a gunny sergeant informs me, "General Kane, most of our artillery portals have run out of juice. All the active ones are off world."

"Then we have to do it the old-fashioned way. Hold off the enemy advance and call-in airstrikes. Hammer these fuckers into the ground. They will not take another inch of this city."

We're going to need jets. All our base's planes are cut off without the portals. The nearest Air Force Base is MATES in San Bernardino. If they're conducting attacks on the alien world, the next nearest base will be Davis Monthan in Arizona.

"Everyone get back into the command center. I want a direct line to MATES and Davis Monthan. We need any jets they have in the air immediately. I want our Air Force to tear these Aliens a new asshole."

Calls are made, while our troops advance into the city.

My orders are to, "Leave the civilian casualties to the city's responders. We can't afford the distractions."

Cecil informs me, "Davis Monthan is scrambling F16s. Estimated time of arrival is one hour."

I am given a direct radio connection to our advancing Marines. "Have you identified the size of the enemy force, Sanchez?"

Captain Sanchez speaks from a radio in a speeding vehicle, the wind interfering with his words. "No…enemy… moving…fast." The familiar sound of a 50-caliber machine gun firing nearby interrupts.

"Do they have vehicles? Over."

"Nnnn—" Then there is only static.

"Say again? Over."

There is no response.

"Shit, someone get me another channel!"

On a new channel, a scared private answers, "Jesus fucking Christ, sir. They're cutting us to fucking pieces."

"Calm down, Marine. You do not have my permission to die yet. Jets are on their way. Can you identify the size of their force?"

He's breathing hard in a clear panic.

"I need to know the size of their force."

He screams as the radio speaker spikes.

"Damnit, what the hell are we up against?!"

The radio comes back on, the private's voice now deadpan. "Are you the one in charge?"

The Anunnaki mouths can't speak but with its powerful telekinetic abilities, it must be manipulating my Marine.

I answer, "Hello, Alien. I assume you've taken my

Marine hostage. You should know we don't negotiate with terrorists."

There is a whimper of pain before the Alien forces the Marine to say, "We are not terrorists. We are the Anunnaki warriors. Your filth destroyed our home world. You are the terrorists."

"Filth is such a simple insult coming from a species that gets off on raping civilians. Marines are trained to fight through the filthiest of conditions. Your handful of ragtag creeps don't stand a chance."

There is a thud and the sound of bones breaking as the private screams in pain. That rattled the Alien real good. It must not be used to trash talk. I feel a slight bit of guilt for the kid he just took his frustration out on.

The voice returns, "Our warriors are ten thousand strong. We cut through your armies on Anun, and we will destroy everything you hold dear on this world. One human at a time. You are filth worth nothing more than the excrement you defecate."

I write on a piece of paper, noting the size of the attacking force and an order to bomb everything, then pass it to Cecil. After a brief moment of shock, he nods understanding before relaying my order to the incoming Air Forces.

I say into the radio, "This is the first time you've fought a resistant enemy, isn't it? Are you even an officer? I bet you're just some pink skinned punk that's never seen real combat. Go get your commanding officer, kid."

"I'll have you know that I am well over fifty of your planet's rotations old, with a lifetime of combat training. Fighting with honor for my people."

For the past ten minutes that I have been having this

conversation, there hasn't been any explosions. I can't help but smile at how easy it is to get under this Alien's gray skin. "Play fighting ain't real fighting, kid. Is this the first time you've been hit back before? You never learned to roll with the punches, did you?" Making my voice as demeaning as possible.

"I will kill you slowly and painfully as you beg me for death over a lifetime of suffering. You will feel the pain of every life you stole from my people." His threats continue on and on.

I turn back to Cecil, who holds up his hand to indicate five minutes until fighter jets arrive.

I hold the speaker up to another to cause feedback to cut off the exaggerated monologue. "Marine, you have my permission to die."

Coughing in pain the Marine yells, "Oorah, sir!" and he pulls the pin on a grenade, cutting off the radio signal with a pop.

The screech of jet's breaking the sound barrier erupt across the sky as missiles are fired into the city, engulfing everything in fire. "Get another round of firebombs on the target. Cecil, you need to pull back."

Red spinning disks cut across all the cars in our parking lot as Aliens rush the base. The spinning blades move almost as fast as bullets, cutting everything in sight to ribbons. As a blade hits fuel, the liquid ignites. Black smoke now blocks out the sun. The base's portal is struck severing our escape to the other side of the country.

I draw my Colt .45, yelling, "Everyone out!"

The window in front of me shatters, peppering everyone

with shards as a gray Anunnaki warrior garbed in a shiny, thin red skin suit floats in. Standing proud, his black eyes scan each of us. The warrior projects its voice into all of our minds, "Primatives!" Then it sends a blade into my assistant while another gets pulled out the second story window by invisible hands.

I fire my gun, only to see the bullet ricochet off a spinning blade. Undeterred, I point my gun downward and blast apart the Alien's foot. It forces a painful screech out of its mouth orifice. As the protective blade spin flutters, I fire another bullet directly into its black eye. Its skull splits wide open as the creature falls to the ground motionless. To be safe, I fire another round splattering its brain matter across the floor.

The average Alien warrior has the ability to block bullets with their blades. According to Yabechun, it takes over a century of training to create a personal forcefield. This was just a low-level grunt. The kid got cocky.

As I pick up one of the silver cylinders containing a deactivated blade, blood drips down my face. The flying glass cut me just next to my old scar. It's not that bad, so I ignore it and reload four rounds into my Colt. I check outside the broken window to see my assistant limping to extraction. Luckily, we weren't on a higher floor. Then he gets sliced in half by the enemy.

Outside, I find a radio operator cowering as the alien weapons slice through our defenses. Forcing the private up, I yell, "Are you in contact with the Air Force?"

Processing his first battle, he nods.

I take the mouthpiece away from him. "This is General

William Kane. We are overrun, Broken Arrow. I say again Broken Arrow."

On the other side, the voice says, "Understood, General."

Expecting that to be the end of the communication, I hear the voice say, "Do you have any parting words for your family, sir?"

There is no time for sentimental words. "No, they already know."

"Come on, Private." I force the frightened kid to move his feet. "Die fighting like a Marine."

I see Cecil as his helicopter lifts off and a red blade cuts off the tail, sending the bird into an uncontrollable spin. It crashes into the ground, sending bodies outward to skid across the concrete. Black smoke from the city fires combined with smoldering debris blocks out the sun.

There is no escape anymore.

I shout to the remaining Marines, a small handful of tired and wounded men mixed into a crowd of noncombatants. "Hold fast. I will not let our end be quiet!"

Mechanics hold rifles for the first time since Basic training years prior. A sad group for a last defiant stand.

Ten gray Anunnaki warriors appear, pushing the dark clouds away with their telekinetic abilities. Their red skin suits remain clean. Each is a head shorter than my six-foot height. Their dark eyes fixed on us show no emotion as forty red blades spin around them.

The one at the center forces his words into my mind. "Is this all your worthless race can muster?"

I shout, "Open fire!" Even in my old age this was how I wanted to go, fighting as a Marine.

My survivors unleash a rain of gun fire. All is blocked by the shield of spinning red blades. I hold my fire, waiting for the moment. A spinning line is not a wall no matter how fast it spins. When I see an exposed shoulder, I fire, taking out the two end Aliens. Eight red blades shoot off, no longer held by Alien's invisible power. Seeing I am the greatest threat, the center Alien sends two of his blades directly at me.

I ignite my stolen sword to deflect the incoming attack. The impact almost breaks my grip. Planting my heels, I remain standing. There is a burning pain in my left thigh and right shoulder. My block saved my life, but I am not unscathed. With a red Xeno blade in my left hand and my family's legacy in my right, I say defiantly, "Is that the best you got?"

The center Alien sends all four of his blades at me first. I attempt to evade and deflect while firing my Colt at the same time. I'm not as fast as I used to be, but my aim has always been true. My shot lands center mass, knocking my foe to the ground, just as a burning heat pierces my side. I have been impaled through my well-worn liver. Dropping to the ground, I feel as if my insides have been flash fried. Air becomes painful to breathe as my lungs are now cooked.

Seven enemy remain in front of us. I refuse to die just yet, firing the last rounds of my Colt from a shaking hand. I need to witness my final victory. I pull the trigger on an empty chamber as the gun slips from my fingers. My strength is now gone.

So this is it…

That revolver has been a part of the Kane family legacy for over a hundred years. Now it could be lost here. I should have given it to my son when I had the chance.

I hear the roaring sound of jets as missiles are fired on my position. "I wonder if I beat my brother to the other side."

My life fades as the world around me erupts with destruction.

CHAPTER 26

TRAVEL

"**J**ASON, WHAT DID THE SOURCE show you?" my father's voice asks.

It takes me a moment to remember where I am. Feels as though it has been years since I breathed the air of the material world. My eyes adjust to the real world. I can see the young soul my father still holds trapped behind his weathered face.

"I know where this is going to end." Standing up, my movement is stiff from laying down for twenty-four hours straight. I almost fall on my mother sleeping on the kitchen bench next to the couch with an open book in front of her.

Thankfully, Dad catches me. He asks, "How much of that tea did you drink?"

I say, "As much as I needed." I adjust my footing to the movement of Mr. Shimizu's RV. In the back, Amy and Judy are sharing the bed. Rick and Zack got stuck in the loft above the cabin. I have to be careful not to step on Alex, laying on the floor because he's too tall to fit anywhere else.

Mr. Shimizu is still driving, now being kept company by Amy's father. I wonder if that old man even sleeps.

"How can you have that much power and you never used it for personal gain?" Amy's father asks.

Mr. Shimizu says, "That is why you will struggle the most to unlock the gifts of the universe. One must learn the responsibility of this power before you can truly unlock it."

"Then explain how those aliens were able to use that exact same power to attack us?" Amy's father asks, expecting there not to be a good answer.

"You can't lose knowledge once it is gained, but you can forget the responsibility of power if you are left unchecked." Mr. Shimizu notices me. "Did you see the end?"

"I did. Sort of. I know I will face the man with red eyes in the ruins of the Vatican, but I can't see past that. Does that mean he's going to kill me?"

Mr. Shimizu says, "Maybe."

My father says, "What do you mean *maybe*? If that's a possibility, then why the heck are we still going to the coast. Let's tell your brother and sister in the car behind us to just stop here."

I say, "Dad, this is all going to end no matter what. If we were to head back home now, destruction will come for us. The man with red eyes does not want loose ends. I have to face him while he's distracted. All of this is my fault. The genocide against an alien race and the death of my friend Angel, as well as his family. I have the power to move objects with my mind and see into the future. I'm probably the only one who can face him. That arrogant bastard has done so much irreparable damage to everyone's lives. I need to put him down, even if that means facing him alone."

Dad says, "You don't have to do anything alone anymore."

I feel his hand gently placed on my shoulder. My body instantly relaxes as just the mere thought of the horror Yabechun has unleashed filled me with a pure hatred. "Thanks, Dad."

We pass a sign that reads Mobile, Alabama. "How exactly are we planning on getting across the Atlantic?"

Mr. Shimizu says, "We'll take a shipping boat. I have a friend that owes me a favor. Commercial flights will be grounded now that the war has reached US soil."

I saw a lot in my trip through the void, but I missed that. "When did that happen?"

Dad says, "About noon yesterday. They took out San Diego. They were talking non-stop on the radio about the general that gave his life to hold back the assault. Hey, Jeff, what was his name again?"

Amy's father says, "General William Kane. I swear that name sounds familiar." He looks off to think.

I swear there is no escaping that family. "Mr. Shimizu, when are you going to help everyone else see The Source?"

Mr. Shimizu says, "Travel across the ocean will take over a month. I will guide those who are willing to make the trip."

Jeff says, "If I wasn't ready, then I would have stayed home in my big comfy chair." He then snaps his fingers with excitement. "I've got it! My eldest had a party at my house a few years back while I was on a business trip. There was a fight in my backyard between a Barry Kane and another teen. So much of my house was wrecked. Thank God, the neighbors called the cops before things got out of hand."

"You are far too eager for power. To gain true power, you

will have to face everything you fear and accept death. Then you will be free to see The Source of all things," Mr. Shimizu says, keeping his eyes on the road.

Eventually, we reach Mr. Shimizu's small home in Florida. My mother pulls me aside with my father and older sister. "Your father and I have been talking with Ann. We don't want to go across the ocean to a battle ground."

"But you've already left Yuma." I am not sure if I want to convince them otherwise.

Mom says, "We did so to protect you. I understand people are looking for you and it was a wise decision with the invasion in California. But I'm not a fighter, never have been."

Ann says, "Listen, little guy. I understand enough to know this is out of my depth. We'll hold down the fort while you guys go do what you believe needs to be done."

I hate it when she calls me *little*. I'm an inch taller than her now. I'd be even taller if not for the drugs in prison, but this is not the time to complain, so I say, "I don't want to lose you again. The war and my imprisonment stole so much of my time with all of you. What if this is the end?"

Dad chimes in, "It ends no matter what, remember. I need to be here to protect them. I trust you are strong enough to not need me now."

He used my own words against me. I share a final embrace with my mother and sister before I leave. Pete comes out of the bathroom just as we head out. "Did I miss something?"

Dad says, "Your mother, sister, and I are staying behind. You have a boat to catch, get going." He doesn't give his eldest son any time to argue, shooing us out the door.

Those of us still willing to make this trip get back in the RV. Mr. Shimizu stops me, holding two padded swords.

Confused, I ask, "What are you doing?"

He tosses one of the padded swords to me. "Show me your skill."

"I see." I don't have any official sword training, just a bit of knife and bayonet training during boot camp in my old life. I look over his elderly physique, seeing nothing special for a man in his seventies. What kind of fight is he going to give me anyway?

Mr. Shimizu takes his stance, sword out front and feet planted. I may not have any special sword training, but I can tell by his stance that he has decades of experience. "Alright, I'll show you exactly what I am capable of."

I extend my consciousness, seeing what Mr. Shimizu's next move will be. He remains firm, no additional images appearing around him. I dart forward with my sword in one hand, my other outstretched. I picture multiple hands holding his weapon in place. He remains still as I prepare to spear him, then at the last moment before I make contact, he turns his body using the held sword to pivot faster. I just barely brush past him. I release his sword from my mental grip, realizing it was used to his advantage. He then moves to strike me behind my head. I try to pull my sword back to block, only to realize it is held in place by Mr. Shimizu's bending of the Source. Then a blunt force smacks the back of my head ever so gently.

Mr. Shimizu holds the padded sword at rest behind my neck. "A fair attempt. You wisely used your gifts from The Source, but you fight with no style." He removes the blade from its killing blow. "I have practiced the way of the sword for five decades. From my studies, I have found the legends of Samurai turned Ronin. A man with red eyes that served the shogun for a hundred years. He would wear fabric over his deformed eyes, fighting blind."

I say sarcastically, "Sounds like my new friend."

"A hundred years of sword fighting experience will be impossible for any swordsman to overcome." He lets go of his padded sword as it floats. Then it hits me in the back of the head again.

Realizing the fight isn't over, I roll away. As I stand back on my feet, the floating sword attacks me. With nothing holding my sword now, I block.

"Your unorthodox fighting style will make counters difficult." His disembodied attack intensifies, keeping me on the defensive.

I once again extend my consciousness to catch the floating sword and throw mine at Mr. Shimizu.

He catches my weapon just as it leaves my hand and smacks me with both swords. "You have a long way to go and not long to get there."

CHAPTER 27

THE NEXT PLANET

THE ANUNNAKI HOME HAS BEEN reduced to a radioactive wasteland. No point in wasting anymore manpower when radioactivity will starve the remaining Xenos. Victory has been secured against the alien armada. Our fleet may have lost eighty five percent of our newly acquired space crafts, but victory is still victory. We move on to the next world of strategic importance. Their warriors' home world, a slightly greater challenge. Gravity is three times greater than ours, and they have battlefield experience. Too bad they had no idea how dirty we can fight.

A thousand more nuclear bombs are detonated across our new target. Population centers burn as we deplete our stockpile of atomic weapons. Watching the mushroom clouds pop up across continents is a beautiful sight. I am grateful to witness this twice within my lifetime.

Yabechun has been held up in the Vatican for the past week since the war started, but he had a Colonel Eagle waiting for me after my first deployment to the alien home world. I am now Colonel Johnathan Kane. He's raising me through the ranks awfully fast. Too bad Barry couldn't wrap his head around that. He doesn't matter anymore. There is no point wasting time on the dead.

After decontamination, I was finally allowed to rest, but I couldn't sleep. I've been deployed before and know real sleep is rare in between the action. You either just lay down with your eyes closed or you wake up every few minutes, expecting something to happen. This feels different, almost as if I have too much energy to actually sleep. Even with the portals allowing for instant travel, I am stuck on post. It has to at least be midnight, so I doubt Vicky is awake to talk.

What would we even talk about?

"How was your day? I had to quarantine an entire regiment because some dumb privates were banging an alien." Then she'd probably complain about the pregnancy and how I should be there. "Sorry, hon, there's a war going on."

All I can do is watch the newsfeed of the bombings on some staticky old television in the barracks on Earth, sitting on the concrete floor with my back rested up against the wall. My large frame doesn't fit the cot I was given, as it was designed for an average person. I've yet to find an accommodation that can fit me now that I am above seven feet tall. I keep scratching at the stump on my right hand while my mechanical arm recharges, It sweats so much in the brace, I think I'm developing a skin rash.

"Where the hell are the other enhanced soldiers? Hercules should at least be here by now. Fucker probably snuck off post for drinks. God damn worthless."

"Colonel Kane?" asks a runner in the darkness.

"What do you want?" I am annoyed by his presence.

"I have a message from General William Kane."

Damn old man stuck in the old ways of doing things. He could just call me, but no, he has to send a handwritten letter. "Is this regarding the San Diego incursion?"

The private says, "I don't know, sir. I didn't read the letter." Then he disappears into the night.

I'm alone again with just the light of the TV to illuminate the small envelope. I am quickly reminded how important a second hand is to open things. Out of frustration, I rip it open with my teeth.

Dear John,

If you are reading this, then I am dead. Take care of your mother. You are now the man of the house. Preserve the legacy of Kane.

William Kane

"That's it?"

The old man was never much for words. I crumple up the letter before tossing it into a nearby waste bin. No point wasting time on the dead.

At 0500, I rise before the sun and reattach my mechanical hand. It still hurts when it connects to the nerve. Then I have to put on a clean jumpsuit for being around radioactive fallout. I don my reenforced armored uniform, now dry after quarantine. It's designed to be easily put on and taken off without assistance. I just have to step into it while sliding under the back protective plate. Then once it is powered on, the advanced armor extends the scales to protect the back of my legs. However, the calf scales keep getting stuck and I have to pull those out manually. The hinges are feeling kind of loose, so I wrap that part in duct tape to secure it. Finally, I grab my helmet before I leave the empty barracks. The base never sleeps as equipment is taken to and from alien worlds for the war. Our drums of war are the roaring sounds of diesel powered engines.

I received my orders from my superior, who is creepily watching the organized flow of military traffic from an officer's quarters. There is a metal refinery on the warriors' planet. They do not specify what kind of metal. I assume it to be the unique alien fuel source, but for all I know it could be for lead. I will be the only enhanced soldier on this mission. James, Igor and Jin have other objectives.

"What about Hercules?"

My superior says, "He was killed in action during the Anunnaki counterattack."

"Are they still advancing across the US? That seems more pressing for an enhanced soldier."

"The enemy is still advancing. We need to take advantage of this opportunity. With their fleet being decimated and their ground forces fading on the primary ruling planet, and while we bombard the warriors' infrastructure, our special forces can take whatever we want. Let the national guard deal with those fuckers on Earth. Our current projections don't see them passing New Mexico. Rednecks from across the country are moving toward the Xeno threat. It will clear the board of the less than desirable. Besides, California has lost most of its use now that we no longer need Hollywood's distractions."

I'm used to dealing with Yabechun's personnel. Black suited men with black sunglasses. I'm almost certain this guy is stationed within the CIA. I wonder when I'll ever get orders from standard military personnel again. Now that I think about it, I think Yabechun is grooming me to be that person. That's what my father was, and now that he's gone... I bet before this war is over, I'll be a General.

All my gear lock and loaded I head for the portal to the alien warrior world. Leaving the comfort of Earth for the increased gravity of a hostile planet entering a nuclear winter. My head set display shows my air filter has twenty-four hours of clean air, my artillery portal has a full battery, and I have plenty of charges. I will have this refinery in less than an hour easily.

On the Alien world a base camp has been set up around the portal. Humans move slow with the increased gravity. While special light weight helicopters have to be used for deployments, a Blackhawk will crumple from its own weight.

I don't need support anymore. I have the combined strength of an entire battalion. Even without the artillery portal on my M249 SAW with a belt fed backpack of a thousand rounds of 5.56x45mm. In the event those run out, I have my reliable MK23 .45 caliber pistol that has never led me astray. I don't need melee weapons anymore, now that I can rip a person in half with my bare hands. I still carry a twelve-inch survival knife as well as a Xeno blade, a spoil from this war.

This world darkens as nuclear dust blocks out its star. As the world falls into shadow the air grows cold, raining radioactive particles. I am dropped a few clicks from the target, an easy run for me now. Where I take up an overwatch position to determine my best route of attack.

The refinery is all but abandoned aside from four warriors forcing a sickly subspecies to work. One of the subspecies falls down, coughing up dark blood. It clambers up and tries to push a container of molten metal with its decaying body. No one stops to help the dying creature, only extending their power to keep the production line moving. Slave labor from an advanced alien species doesn't make sense. This process should easily have been automated by an interplanetary civilization.

Upon closer look with my scope, I see that the subspecies is almost human. A mix between human and Anunnaki. Fully formed ears and mouths but hairless, flaking skin. Tanned skin, probably from over exposure to vitamin D. Now it clicks. When they collect humans, it's not just for pleasure but for a work force. How many people have they really taken? Yabechun never gave an exact number, though he tracks everything. Even if all the missing people both reported and unreported were in fact alien abductions, it couldn't be enough to sustain a slave economy of a multi planet civilization. Their abductions still have to compete with human crime, and humans are far too active in the underground to be second best at hurting ourselves.

I track one of the Anunnaki warriors as it tosses the latest overworked slaves onto a pile of corpses. The pile consists of the human hybrids as well as dozens of other mixed species. Some have burned feathers, lizard scales, abnormal skeletal structures closer to lemurs. I see tails and even tentacles. There appears to be at least a dozen different species. How many planets do they steal lives from, or are these the result of something else?

That's not important. I take aim at the most senior Anunnaki, garbed in a jumpsuit with many colorful patterns to signify rank. The standard foot soldier jumpsuit typically consists of one to two colors with no pattern. It is also the only Xeno I have seen with visible wrinkles on its gray skin.

Resting the barrel of my gun on a secure cover overlooking the refinery, I control my breathing and then gently squeeze the trigger. A quick burst of bullets peppers the Anunnaki, ending the lives of the unprepared foot soldiers. The senior warrior stands firm, the bullets meant for him floating frozen in the air, smashed against an invisible forcefield.

I immediately fire artillery munitions from my portal, only to see the large round spin around the warrior before being slingshot back at me. I dive out of the way as the round explodes. The shockwave knocks the wind out of me I feel my internal organs shift. The artillery round has made the ground unstable. Before I can regain my balance, I drop to the refinery's primary work floor with a hard landing. Coughing, I try to focus my breathing.

The slaves try to run but stop as a nonverbal shout is forced into all of our heads. "Do not stop working!" says a warrior calmly floating from its perch above the primary work floor.

I should not have been able to hear that. Is my helmet compromised? Then I feel a chunk of metal stuck in my helmet. It scratches against the side of my head. I'm lucky it didn't go any farther.

The Anunnaki Warrior begins to ignite his four red blades, spinning them around him. I open fire, hoping to hit him before he can attack, while sending a signal through my portal to change ammunition.

The Elder Warrior projects its words into my mind. "So this is the best humans have to offer? Here I hoped for a real fight."

I fire an artillery shell at my enemy. Chlorine gas engulfs the being. Taking that as my cue, I run for better terrain.

The warrior pushes the gas outward before safely inhaling, then projects its thoughts outward to all. "You'll have to do better than cheap tricks."

I keep firing Chlorine gas bombs as I run, filling the large room with yellow gas and cutting off its vision. Unfortunately, the only coughing is from the slaves as they succumb to the chemical weapons.

The Anunnaki Warrior keeps the gas at bay with its red blades spinning outward. It doesn't have me zeroed, but it hits close to home, slicing open my backpack full of ammo. I quickly unbuckle the straps as the gunpowder in the round are ignited by the blade's heat. Tossing it at my enemy, I watch as the Xeno catches the rounds with its telekinetic force field. Then I fire an artillery round at the pack and take cover just as the explosion rockets out shrapnel.

The words, "Not bad, human," are projected into my mind. There stands the Anunnaki Warrior, only slightly burned and a small handful of minor lacerations bleeding across its skin. "I have not trained my power for over five hundred of your planet's rotations to simply lose." It smiles before sending all four of its blades at me.

I dodge them, firing the last few rounds in my Saw. The bullets bounce off its telekinetic shield.

This approach isn't working. I send a signal through my portal before tossing my rifle to the ground in between us. Standing up straight, I take out my claimed Xeno sword and my twelve-inch steel knife. "Let's have a real fight them."

The Anunnaki warrior recalls all four of his blades back to him, holstering two while catching two in its hands. It takes a firm stance, blades pointed at me.

I mimic the stance with my knife out front.

The Anunnaki Warrior begins his approach, blades held tight. I hold firm, waiting for the Xeno to get close, hoping his desire for an honorable fight will bring him to me. He passes my rifle on the ground, and I smile just to have that wiped from my face as the Xeno attacks. Its blades clash with mine, slicing my steel knife in half. I toss the remaining hilt at the Xeno. It impacts my enemy right in the chest but does not stick without a tip. The Anunnaki Warrior looks shocked that its force field did not stop it. Then I bring down my stolen blade only to have it blocked. The Anunnaki Warrior has to use both blades to hold me back. My smile grows as fear fills my enemy. I kick the Xeno hard in the chest, sending it back to my discarded rifle. The Anunnaki Warrior tries to catch itself, only to stumble to the ground, its breath erratic.

"Sarin gas is clear and odorless. Causes all your muscles to tense uncontrollably."

The Anunnaki Warrior violently coughs up dark liquid matching it's blood. It drops it deactivated weapons.

I bring down my blade, slicing The Anunnaki Warrior's head from its shoulders. I say, "First rule of combat, there are no rules in combat." Then I crush the skull beneath my boot, sending its brain matter outward.

I send the signal through my portal to stop the Sarin gas. Thankfully, my filters were not compromised. With another blade to add to my collection, I call in, "This is Omega One, priority target has been eliminated and the refinery is all clear. Over."

Home base answers, "We read you, Omega One. We are sending in evac with reinforcements to fortify the zone."

I reply, "Roger that, I'll sit tight. Over and out."

While sitting down to catch my breath, I dislodge the metal shard from my helmet and apply a strip of duct tape over the breach. It's difficult to place the tape with my mechanical hand. Tape and gloves never work well together. I won't be able to get a replacement for a while, so this will have to do.

Now that the room is secured, I look over the pile of corpses. Mutated creatures that once worked this refinery. Some have exoskeletons similar to insects. Reminds me of playing with bugs when I was a kid. Barry and I had a gross out war, leaving stink bugs and wolf spiders in each other's beds. Had to put an end to it when Mom found a tarantula while doing laundry. We blamed it on Austin, getting everyone in trouble. That was a long time ago. No point in thinking about that now. There will be another mission, more targets to eliminate before my day is done.

CHAPTER 28

THIS IS NO CRUISE

FOCUS, JASON, LET YOUR MIND perceive the world beyond this moment. Inhale in the salty ocean air. Feel the shipping barge sway in the waves. Do not let your last meal betray you at this moment. Exhale, allowing your muscles to relax but not enough to lose this fight.

Surrounded by five attackers all armed with a sword same as me, I take another controlled breath and get into the stance Mr. Shimizu taught me. Feet planted firm with both hands on my padded sword in front of me, I say, "I will win this time."

We stand atop the stacks of shipping containers on the barge's deck. Rick, Zack, Alex, my brother Pete, and Mr. Shimizu are all ready to strike me. Mr. Shimizu and I both have telekinetic abilities, but only I can glimpse into the future without psychedelic aid.

I extend my consciousness into The Source of all things to see who will attack first. Rick will make the first move from my right side in five seconds, followed by Zack on the left. My stomach starts to gargle as my head begins to feel dizzy. I am not letting sea sickness beat me this time.

Rick takes a step toward me, but I push him back with my mind before Zack attacks from the left. I block his attack, pulling him off balance with my power as I deliver a slash to his gut with my padded sword. Alex and Pete attack next, at the same time. I hold Pete's foot in place, causing his swing to be horribly off balance and with one foot held in place he fall into the splits. He yells out several rude words. Alex almost stabs me, but I duck under his reach just in time. I roll away, smacking his shin with my sword followed by a blow to his back to finish him. Then my sword is held in the air by Mr. Shimizu. I stretch my mind to push him just as his sword flies at me. I clash with the floating weapon, trying to predict its next move only to be attacked by Rick at the same time. Now, defending against two attackers is already difficult. Alex hops over not yet defeated. I pull him into Rick, causing them to fall over each other. Just to be smacked by Pete now angry from his fall. I need to look into the future and push at the same time if I hope to win, but it's all too much to focus on while in combat. I try to push Mr. Shimizu down again, but he holds firm as I am driven back.

Unfortunately, I remember my footing just as I'm about to step off the edge of the shipping container. Trying to fix my feet and not fall of the high perch, I yelp as the padded sword hits me on the head. Falling, I extend my consciousness to grab hold of the container's edge. Instead, I swing as if from a rope, into the side of the metal container with a loud clang before landing hard on a steel walkway below.

My stomach now sees I have been weakened and chooses this moment to attack as well. I hurl my last meal over the side of the boat. My legs are shaky from an exhaustive work-out, and I hold onto the side railing for dear life.

Mr. Shimizu shouts down to me, "That's enough for the day, Jason. We'll try again in the morning."

I answer with a thumbs up while clutching the side rail.

After emptying the contents of my stomach again, I make my way to the living quarters of the ship. Mr. Shimizu leads everyone who just beat me in a post workout stretch. I retrieve an ice pack from the fridge. Placing it on my shoulder, I realize I definitely pulled something when I fell. We've been on this boat for only three days so far and it feels as if I'm getting hurt more than gaining skills.

The crew of the ship pay us almost no mind. They probably think we're some kind of cult the captain owes. In a way, we kind of are. Mr. Shimizu has been preparing everyone to enter into The Void. If they are not ready to experience death, then they will not return. I had accepted my own death years ago, and witnessing the other side with a psychedelic aid felt natural. I will help Mr. Shimizu guide them as best I can, but it will ultimately be up to them whether they choose to come back to reality.

I need them all to make it through. The man with red eyes is not someone to face without power. In the void, I watched him run faster than sound and splat a living being with one punch. Not to forget that he took a killing blow from a weapon I know to have the power to cut steel as if it were butter. I will end him by my own hands and make things right for once. He killed all those alien creatures by removing their heads. He's more like them than he wants to admit. That's how I'll end the horror of his existence. Death is all he deserves now.

Tomorrow night we shall share a bitter tea laced with psychedelics. Mr. Shimizu has had everyone on a very particular diet to cleanse the body of unnatural foods. Unfortunately, this diet has done nothing for my sea sickness. Even on a massive boat, my stomach hates the waves.

After our dinner of fresh fruits and vegetables directly from Mr. Shimizu's garden, we head to our quarters. It's a good thing we can go back to normal food soon, because these vegetables are no longer very fresh.

Almost everyone else has to live in shared quarters consisting of bunk beds closer to coffins. I lucked out and got my own room. A tiny space directly next to the communal bathroom consisting of a bed just big enough for one. Reminds me of my prison cell.

Someone beat me to the shower. To kill time, I take out the alien cylinder I've kept in the drawer under the bed. It's been feeling lighter. Holding the switch, I extend the blade. It glows red, radiating a passive heat and giving off a gentle hum. I give the blade a twirl, coming to rest in a prepared stance with both hands on the hilt. With a deep breath, I extend my consciousness to make the active blade float in front of me. I begin to spin it slowly, picking up speed but nowhere near what that alien did in the desert.

"That's a neat trick," says a voice from my doorway.

The blade instantly deactivates as my concentration is interrupted. The cylinder flies into the wall before ricocheting onto my small bed. I spin around, trying to act naturally.

Amy is standing there in nothing but a towel.

I feel my face turning red as I try to look up and away. "So the shower is open now," I quip, trying to play it cool.

She says, "It is, but I wanted a moment with you." She closes the door behind her. "In private."

My heart rate skyrockets. I don't need powers to see what she is implying. I have zero idea how to proceed here. "Oh! Uhhhh," just kind of stumbles out of my mouth.

Amy says, "I've always had a little crush on you. When I saw you beat up Dylan and his goons, I kind of fell in love with you." The towel drops, revealing her naked body. "Thank you for taking me on a real adventure."

She takes my hand and places it on her breast, before kissing me with a passion I didn't know was possible. I want nothing else at this moment besides her. As we lay upon the small bed embracing each other in what I can only describe as a furious love, I feel complete.

I fall asleep holding Amy in my arms that night, dreaming of peace for the first time, only to be woken up by someone banging on my door.

"Get up, Jason!"

Amy and I rush to get dressed.

I shout, "Just a minute."

The person continues impatiently banging on the door.

I open the door as Amy tries to hide out of view. Pete stands there with two padded swords. "Get out to the deck, now," he demands before stomping away.

Relieved, I say, "I thought it was your father."

Amy says, "Me too."

"I guess I better go." Before I leave, I kiss her on the lips. "We'll talk later."

She shouts, "Don't fall off the boat," as I hurry to the deck.

On the open deck, I find Pete pacing at the bow of the

ship. "What's going on? I was kind of in the middle of something." Probably not my best choice of words, but he doesn't know that.

Pete throws a padded sword at me. "Defend yourself!" Then he rushes to attack.

There is no time to clear my head and focus my powers, forcing me to rely on the instinct gained in combat. My brother shows no mercy as he strikes. I deflect to create an opening and thrust forward, hitting him in the chest.

Pete says, "Damnit, Jason. How are you this good? Are you using your powers?"

"No, that was skill. This is power." I hover the sword just above my palm. "What's got you in such a bind?"

"This ain't natural."

I catch the hilt. "It's actually quite natural. You'll understand once you see The Source of all things." I return my weapon to on guard.

He replies to my challenge with a wide swing. "I don't think I will. All of this is too much for me."

I almost miss the block. "What?"

Pete dodges my first swing. "Jason, this is all beyond me. I studied Criminal Justice in college to become a lawyer. Not this crazy shit." He catches my next strike with his hand. "You came back from the dead with fucking superpowers. Then the world goes to war with aliens, and you plan to fight some fucking immortal demigod man with a space sword."

I say, "To be fair, I never actually died. It was a government coverup."

He lets go of the padded sword. "That's exactly what I'm talking about! How can you not see how insane that is? Five days ago, most of the world made sense. I don't want to see anymore." He turns away to look over the ship's railing.

Seeing that our sparring is over, I lean against the railing next to him and look out at the ocean. We stay there in silence for a while.

Pete finally says, "Your imprisonment and diagnosis destroyed Mom and Ann. Dad didn't speak for months after your sentence. Seeing you closer to death every weekend was impossible to bear. The hardest thing was just how quiet everything was, as if the world had lost its sound. Now…it's almost too loud."

"I'm sorry. I didn't know what was happening outside of confinement. I robbed everyone of a normal life."

Pete turns to me. "Will fighting this guy fix anything?"

Will it? Murder won't bring back Angel's family. Yet what Yabechun has done can't be allowed to continue. He'll come for my family as soon as he completes the destruction of the Alien world. Or if the Alien world killer wins, then someone will have to finish the fight against that monster.

I say, "It will bring an end one way or another."

Pete says, "Could you not say such cryptic shit. Listen, I have your back, but for crying out loud, just talk normal."

I say, "I'm cryptic because I don't have the answer. What I do know is that all of this ends in the ruins of Vatican City. I don't even know if I will win, just that this will be the end."

"And I will be there with you just as your brother. Not with this weird shit."

I want to argue about how out classed we'll be otherwise. Instead, I accept it, because if Pete really believes he's not ready, forcing him into the void would have a negative result. "Alright, just keep an eye on us. The crew seems cool, but it's probably wise to have a sober outlook."

We return to the living quarters where everyone is just kind of hanging out. Amy's father Jeff is reading a small red book. I can't see the title. Judy watches Rick and Zack play a game of foosball against Alex and Amy. I catch Amy's eye, allowing Zack to score a goal. He over exaggerates his celebration by pretending there is a huge crowd watching.

Judy says, "Chill, dude, you're still five points behind."

Zack finishes his celebration with a high five to Alex. "I will enjoy any victory over Rick no matter how small. He's too good at games like this."

Rick says, "It's called talent."

Amy leaves the game to greet me with a private whisper in my ear, "Can we talk?"

Pete immediately walks away, and I hear Rick loudly whisper, "I knew it! Pay up."

Zack begrudgingly hands over a crumpled up five-dollar bill. "Damnit."

Amy pulls me out of the room. "We didn't really talk much after last night, before your brother pulled you away."

I hold her close, not wanting to ever let her go. "I don't really know what to say. I've lived so many short lives. None of them brought me back to you. Now I feel as though there is nowhere else I should be."

She kisses me on the lips before saying, "That is the most romantic thing anyone has ever said to me."

"Really? I thought I was rambling a bit."

"The last jackass I dated never shared how he felt. Only ever texted me the word *bone* with a question mark." She grimaces, reliving the event. "Not like you. You're taking me to the other side of the world."

"This will be dangerous, but I promise no matter what, I will not let any harm come to you or anyone else." I vow my soul at this moment.

"It is time," announces Mr. Shimizu as he places tea out.

Before I let go of Amy, I ask, "Are you sure you want to see into The Void?"

"Will you be with me?"

"Of course."

"Then I am ready."

We all drink the laced tea and lie down in the breakroom. The shell that is Jason Baker falls away as do his worldly desires, replaced only with the vast emptiness that is The Void between all things.

CHAPTER 29

ANOTHER OBJECTIVE

"**T**HIS IS COLONEL JOHNATHAN KANE. The stronghold has been cleared. All Anunnaki have been eliminated. Over," I convey to command as I stand outside what was once an well-fortified hold out for remaining Xenos. The construction reminds me of a castle. Tall stone walls with spires that look out into what was once a vast wilderness. Now the trees are burned to broken husks.

I understand why I was sent to deal with these few holdouts. The killing of powerful Anunnaki Warriors is something only an enhanced soldier can do without large casualties. In this world, they are closer to warlords. Those with the most power rule. The commander of this castle was just like the one at the refinery, able to catch bullets with its mind and could even turn back my artillery shots. Couldn't send in aircraft since they could be pulled from the sky. Regular infantry would have their weapons turned on them. This was a mission only I could do. I'm maneuverable enough to dodge any returned attack. I wasn't able to rely on sarin gas this time. Had to get creative, so I used one of the subspecies slaves as a shield and then cut through both with my stolen blade. Their invisible shield doesn't work once it catches something and a hole is created to hold that object. That was a gamble that paid off.

This target took too long. Punctured my suit and cracked the lance on my mask. Gonna have to keep using duct tape until I can return to post. I don't know how resistant I am to radiation. Should be fine as long as I keep my exposure short. Almost ninety percent of this planet's surface is contaminated after the bombing.

While drinking from the built-in straw in my mask, I hear command reply, "We read you, Colonel. Escort is on the way. Resupply before your next objective."

The water goes down the wrong pipe, causing me to cough uncontrollably before I can respond in a hoarse voice, "Roger that."

"By the way, Colonel Kane, I was told to inform you that your son was born a few hours ago."

Have I really been gone that long? "Thank you. Over."

I am alone for miles on this desolate planet, accompanied only by the cold of this world. The star is blocked out by thick clouds of ash. The castle crumbles from my attack. I left nothing alive within these grounds. My son was born billions of miles away. He will be named William after my father, but I'll call him Bill to keep them separate.

The dual propellers of a V-22 Offspring lands nearby.

The mission comes first.

We still don't have enough alien crafts to use for troop deployment. I board the vessel and resupply for my next encounter. I'm able to take off my mask and helmet during transport. Finally able to wipe away the sweat, I devour several MREs. This body requires lots of fuel now. I attach fresh filters for a new gasmask, collect more ammo for my Saw, and replace the battery on my artillery portal.

My next objective is another stronghold. Another elder to eliminate. Are we out of nukes? Maybe Yabechun is testing the full capabilities of this investment.

It doesn't matter…I have a job to do.

I am dropped off several miles from the next stronghold. This one is built into the side of a cliff. I could just bombard this place, but I need to confirm the kill. The stone doors are wide open, a clear invitation. I walk in with a weapon at the ready. The inside is carved from the rock to create a great hall with a crystal chandelier giving off a bright light to this elegant room. Bodies of subspecies lay in bloody bits across the floor, the smell of other bodily fluids strong enough to pierce my filters.

An Anunnaki Elder Warrior sits in a large stone chair. This one does not wear clothes. Its gray body is splashed with the blood of its slaughtered slaves. Its wrinkled head rests on one hand. It projects, "The end of days has come, human," into my mind.

Out of curiosity, I glance between its legs. Alien genitalia is disgustingly similar to our own. I have no clever words to share with this creature. It is clear he cares for nothing anymore, so I simply say, "As does all things." I shoulder my rifle, knowing bullets will do no good here. I ignite my claimed Xeno blade.

The Anunnaki stands, igniting its own blade. "An honest duel to the death. I've dreamed of this day."

I charge as the Anunnaki soars into the air. I grab the torso of a dead something, throwing it at my descending enemy. He comes down to deal an overhead strike easily blocked by my own blade just as the corpse hits his invisible telekinetic shield. In that moment, I punch through the dead body to impact the Elder Warrior's sternum, shattering the bones that protect its internal organs. He drops his blade and falls to the ground gasping for air. I deliver a hard stomp, splattering its brains across the stone floor.

I inform my commander, "Another target eliminated. Awaiting new orders."

Soon I am delivered to my next target, a mansion on top of a mountain. The mansion is of a design I have never seen before. Too futuristic to seem Victorian, yet somehow old fashioned. Large bay windows with metal sidings cut to simulate wooden planks.

As I prepare to enter the massive building, a voice is projected into my head. "Over here, human." The internal voice directs me to a bench overlooking the cliffside. An Anunnaki sits peacefully soaking in the view. "Please, I wish for you to see this."

I approach slowly, my SAW ready to fire the instant this thing tries to catch me off guard. Nothing happens when I reach the bench. I remain behind the Anunnaki, my rifle pointed at its head.

"It's quite the view, isn't it?" The Anunnaki gestures to the embers of a city with a massive crater in the center. Every building has fallen down either from the blast or fire damage. "I remember when we did the same to your world."

My gun still pointed at my enemy, I say, "I thought your people only lived for a few hundred years, not twelve thousand."

He leans back to look me in the eye. His red cat-like

eyes are eerily similar to Yabechun's. "I was in my adolescence when we unlocked the means to unnaturally extend our lives. As the offspring of our emperor, I would gain the throne upon his passing but with everlasting life, an heir to the throne was no longer needed. Then with a failed coup, I was banished to this world of primitive warriors."

"I'm not here for your life story."

He returns to gazing out over the valley. "I know, but I want someone to know my story before the end. It was far too long of a life for it to just vanish. Besides, you wield one of my creations on your belt. I designed the Anunnakien sword to kill my immortal father. Now it will be used against me. How ironic."

I ask, "Will you resist?"

He shakes his head. "I will not if you would please share your name with me."

"John Kane."

"Man of an evil marking. I hope you find peace before the end reaches your home."

"My people are nowhere near our end."

The Anunnaki lets out bits of broken breaths resembling laughter. "You may have beaten my people today. You may even drive us to extinction, but others will now rise in this galaxy. The species we have kept at bay will now expand with inventions more devastating than your own. Your portal technology will be replicated by others. There is sentient fungus that can consume a planet if not kept at bay. Mechanical beings that have achieved consciousness without emotions, only calculated consumptions. There are insects that can travel between planets without technology, just their eggs shot beyond their atmosphere, yet still connected to a hive mind. All of which my people have kept contained to their solar systems. Now it will be your turn." He stands up to face me. "That is, if you can survive our greatest weapon."

He projects images of an Anunnaki torn apart by thousands of battles, but each injury makes it stronger. Its body dwarfs me in size, and it radiates a telekinetic force that smashes solid rock without effort. A breathing natural disaster. I see it kill all life on a planet of humanoid reptiles. They use weapons of combustion similar to ours, but in mere months, this monster eliminates all life on a planet of a billion.

"Tell me, John Kane, do you believe your people can face our greatest weapon?"

I stow my fear, remembering the great feats I've see Yabechun achieve. He has broken the sound barrier just by running. Flipped a tank one handed with ease. Survived a thousand nuclear bomb tests during the Cold War. Even now at the peak of my strength, I stand no chance against him. "Our leader is stronger than your monster."

"Maybe, but I doubt—"

I fire a bullet into the Anunnaki's skull, then chop off its head before kicking it into the valley below. "I don't doubt him." After I collect myself, I radio in, "Command, target eliminated. Awaiting new orders."

CHAPTER 30

BATTLE BETWEEN GODS

A SPACECRAFT HOVERS JUST INSIDE THE atmosphere, plotting the best landing location to cause the most damage. Then the decision is made for it by a squadron of jets firing supersonic missiles that force the craft on a new trajectory. The disk spirals down to Earth's surface, demolishing buildings as it tumbles. It destroys modern tourist attractions in an ancient city until it rolls to a stop in Saint Peter's Square with just enough momentum to topple the Vatican Obelisk.

Vatican City is still scarred from the rabid Anunnaki many months ago. No doubt there will be even less standing this time as the two greatest living weapons stand to battle on once holy ground.

The Holy City is empty aside from one man standing at the threshold of Saint Peter's Basilica. His red goat-like eyes remained fixed on the crash site as he straightens his black suit and tie and then walks down the old steps he once loathed, for that is where he watched his wife die. The very steps where he killed his best friend. His dress shoes thump against the stone ground. A steam valve breaks as the spacecraft attempts to open. Angered by the inconvenience, the single passenger punches the door off, sending the silver slab of metal speeding toward the Basilica. The man with red eyes tilts his head to the left ever so calmly as the metal slab nearly misses him.

From the broken craft, a large gray monstrous alien being steps out dressed in a barbaric garb of dried skins collected from conquered worlds. Its massive muscles pulsate with a fury ready to destroy another civilization. The face is blank as the monster releases a telekinetic screech powerful enough to crack the ground. A mortal man would die of a cerebral hemorrhage but not Yabechun. He stops a mere ten paces from this beast and locks his red eyes with the monster's own red eyes, as it towers five feet above the earthling.

Yabechun says plainly, "This world doesn't end until I say it ends."

The monster darts forward, cracking the sound barrier in a single bound as it lands a solid punch. The impact unleashes a shockwave powerful enough to shatter windows four hundred yards away. Yabechun is sent flying back into the Basilica and out the other side, destroying solid travertine stone walls before he finally skids to a stop half a mile away.

The silence of the abandoned city is undercut by laughter, glorious and loud. Then Yabechun shouts, "I actually felt that!" He rises back to his feet, brushing the debris from his tattered suit. "I haven't been able to feel in over sixty years!" He sprints back to the square, hurtling through the holes he just made and pulling stray bits of stone behind him in a vortex of speed, to deliver a punch with a thunderous crack.

The monster takes the impact to the lower gut with enough force to lift off the ground and smash into its own crashed ship, breaking metal. The monster tumbles over and on to its knees, and a clear liquid spills from the orifice that constitutes its mouth.

Yabechun pushes the spacecraft debris away with one hand. "Don't tell me that's all you got? You're supposed to be my equal. Can't you heal back stronger from almost any wound? Or was that really the best you had?"

The alien beast wipes away the liquid, projecting all of its malice into Yabechun's mind. It creates a telekinetic field that shatters the street and lifts the stone around the two.

Yabechun smiles crooked teeth. "You'll have to do better than that." He pushes back with images from the Anunnaki genocide.

The beast launches itself at Yabechun. However, this time Yabechun answers with his own attack. The two clash fists, igniting the air in between them and causing a powerful blast. Neither back down, only exchanging more blows, ripping apart the ground around them, until a crater is left in their wake.

In the midst of the exchange, the monster focuses all its inherent power behind its fist, delivering an uppercut that sends Yabechun into the sky. Then with its extendable consciousness, it grabs the human and throws him back to the Basilica, smashing the roof to bits with one projectile.

Yabechun is given no time to stand as he is thrown back out of the Basilica and collides with what was once the art museum. As he rallies himself after having his head rocked, the monster alien begins pulling the Basilica apart, sending large chunks of travertine stone flattening the area. When almost nothing is left of the Basilica but ruin, Yabechun bursts from the rubble and grabs the beast by the ankle, pulling it off balance and into a spin. Building momentum, he sends the alien out of the remains of Vatican City and into the remains of Rome.

The fight between these two unstoppable forces decimates what has stood for over two thousand years. Every blow cracks like thunder, and neither opponent shows any sign of fatigue as each wound heals in mere moments. The battle rages for hours between these two immortal beings. The sun sets and rises before Yabechun feels an odd itch in his side. When he looks down, he sees a marble sword piercing his left side. Must have happened when he flew into a statue. He is unable to remove it as the alien beast's massive hand grabs his face, forcing him into another fountain.

The water has a familiar taste of another time. Yabechun takes this moment to pull the stone sword from his body, then stabs it into the beast's forearm, ripping the tendons that allow for grip. Yabechun jumps out of the water, landing on the broken decorative statues surrounding the old fountain. He notices his side does not instantly close, and neither does the beast's forearm.

He says, "We're finally hitting our limits."

Yabechun shoots across the fountain just in time for the alien to see a black figure heading toward its head. The beast strikes the shadow only for it to of been Yabechun's black coat. A blow to its knee rips apart the supporting tissue, dropping the beast to one working leg. Not done, Yabechun throws a punch with all his strength behind it only to have his fist caught. Before he pulls away, the beast slams his elbow down, snapping Yabechun's arm so his fingers touch his shoulder with a cruel twist.

Only one grunt of agony is made before Yabechun breaks free and delivers a hard hit to the alien's genitals. The beast gives zero indication of any pain.

As he tries to straighten out his misshapen right arm, Yabechun grumbles, "Should have expected that."

The beast charges, hopping on its working leg. Yabechun uses his enemy's momentum to perform a judo throw. As the monster bounces off the hard ground, it unleashes a psychic blast that pushes Yabechun back, crushing his internal organs.

Blood seeps through Yabechun's gritted teeth as he forces himself to remain on his feet. The alien lands a sloppy hit as it tries to get up. Yabechun remains unmoving until a second-strike lands, then he reaches forward and clamps his fingers around the beast's long neck. He squeezes as the alien delivers a barrage of attacks. Fists land with concussive shock waves as an unseeable power presses Yabechun outward, yet the man from Earth does not waver as his grip tightens.

Yabechun has forgotten his intellect, only focused on the task at hand. "Crush."

He takes a step forward, his one arm still tight as the beast continues its desperate assault. Then with another step, forward his vision begins to blur. In unrelenting furry, he yells, "This is my planet!" He takes off in a full sprint, pushing the alien through the remaining stone buildings.

Unable to stop the push on one leg, the beast grabs at anything that could help and smashes stones against his enemy. Then it finds a jagged piece of rebar and stabs it through Yabechun's bicep. The protrusion severs a tendon, breaking his grip just enough for the beast to pull free and toss the human away before falling to the ground. It lies there, trying to catch its breath for just a moment.

The battle has brought the alien monster back to its crashed ship in Saint Peter's Square. The beast rubs at its crushed breathing pipe, feeling a new level of pain it had not felt in millennia, and fear.

Focused upon leaving, the alien does not notice the human sneaking up behind him. Yabechun tosses his tie around the Beast's neck, pulling it tight with one partially working hand and his foot against the monster's back.

The tie cuts through the beast's throat far too easily. It has been lined with a thin metal wire, a unique alloy that can cut through stone if pressure is applied properly.

The beast claws at the tightening string, unable to get its fingers underneath it and only doing more damage to itself. It attempts to turn around to get at its enemy to no avail. Even psychic blasts do nothing as each push fades to be weaker than the last.

Darkness enters the monster's eyes for the first time in centuries. The void of nothing, pulling him back. He desperately searches for any memory that could help. All the other battles were one sided and he could easily wipe out all life on a planet. Not even his earliest memory in the pod, as his skin was peeled off for the operation that turned him into this unstoppable force. It was supposed to make him immortal, yet death has come.

The beast's head pops off as Yabechun pulls his tie away. Then with one final stomp he crushes the Anunnaki's greatest living weapon brain into a splattered paste.

Yabechun stands victorious, breathing hard for the first

time in many years. He looks upon his greatest victory. His oldest enemies have finally fallen. The final remains of Rome have been smashed to rubble. The religious city dedicated to undermining him has been robbed of all value and purpose. As the monsters that created him burn light years away. Their greatest weapon has been defeated. While his men claim the resources that gave the Anunnaki power in the galaxy for him. What could possible stand against his now growing empire?

I stand alone now ready to face this immortal man.

He doesn't look, already knowing I am here. His words are cold. "Jason Baker, are you sure you want it to end here?"

CHAPTER 31

MAN AGAINST GOD

STAND TALL, MY BODY REBUILT back to its prime. My mind is one with The Source of all things, surrounded by the ruins of history. Vatican City and the surrounding remains of Rome were reduced to rubble from the great battle to the death between demigods.

The man with red eye's stands above his defeated adversary. His right arm bent backwards and twisted incorrectly. His formal suit has been reduced to tattered rags. He tosses his tie aside, the tool of his great victory. "It's over, Jason. My Magnum Opus has been achieved. Humanity can now take our rightful place in this galaxy without religious interference."

I ignite my claimed Anunnaki blade, glowing red with heat. "Not with you." Beginning my calm approach, I keep my heart rate low.

Seeing the intent in my eyes, he attempts to straighten out his disfigured right arm. Amidst the pops of his broken bones, I send my blade flying at him. He moves his neck just enough to avoid a lethal strike, but the weapon still manages to sever his shoulder muscle.

"You foolish child!" His face is red with exhausted anger.

Returning the blade to my hand, I say, "It has to end here." Now I'm close enough to attack at close range.

Yabechun is still fast enough to dodge my attacks but only just barely. The tip of my blade manages to skim his flesh, leaving small cuts across his bruised body. He remains nimble while trying to take something out of his right pocket with his left hand.

As he dodges one of my attacks, he turns to deliver a spinning back kick. The blow hits a telekinetic barrier I prepared, sparing me any great damage, but it still sends me toppling backward.

He finally pulls the silver cylinder from his pocket. "I warned you, boy."

He ignites his own red blade.

"Why didn't you use that against the Monster Anunnaki?" I say, antagonizing his incompetence.

Yabechun takes up a left-handed fencing stance. "That had to be completed with my own hands to send a message of my power."

"Yet you're going to die to an unstable mortal delinquent."

While telekinetically throwing rubble from the destroyed landscape, I attack with my weapon. Our blades clash with thunder. His strength has been taxed to its limit, so now he is on my level. Then I see his right arm returning to its proper shape. I jump back as he tries to grab me, using my power to throw blood from the nearby alien corpse in his eyes. In the brief moment he is blinded, I dart low, slicing his stomach open, and then follow up with a strike to the back of his neck.

My blade is deflected. He stands ready, still without his vision and now one hand holding his stomach closed. He silently waits for me. I toss a stone to confuse him, but he remains motionless. I begin to spin my blade with my mind before sending it straight for his head.

Yabechun deflects the blade, sending it into the air.

"No way, I call bullshit!"

He wipes his eyes clear. "The blade makes a unique humming sound, kid." His stomach wound slowly closing.

I'm running out of time. I have to finish this now. I summon all the power I have gained to hold him in place while I attack. After a clash with his blade, I deliver a solid slash across his arm. He looks confused at how I managed that. I attack again after another three clashes, this time slicing through his quad.

"How?" He's annoyed I've bested him twice.

I don't answer. Seeing his next move will give me the perfect counter. Another clash allows me to slice his stomach open once again. As he drops, I bring my blade down upon his head.

Releasing my rage upon my enemy. "It's over!"

He blocks, simultaneously delivering an open palm strike to my solar plexus that sends me flying backward. I roll to a stop, my body scrapped up by the exposed rubble.

Yabechun rises back to his feet still pushing his guts back inside his body. "Now it's over." His face is not angry anymore. He looks tired of all of this. Tired of the constant fighting. Tired for his extended life. He walks toward me, switching the blade to his right hand. "That was a good try…"

The wind is knocked out of me. I struggle for breath as I search for my blade. *Where did it go?*

"But you never stood a chance."

I see the Anunnaki cylinder on the ground behind Yabechun.

"A lone man is not enough."

I force myself to push all the air out of my lungs and catch my breath, then extend my consciousness to pull the cylinder to me.

Yabechun freezes as an unseen forces holds him in place, unable to move before the cylinder hits his back. Then I ignite the blade. Sending the point through his heart and popping out his chest. His body folds as his spinal cord is severed, and he drops his own Anunnaki blade.

I pick up his deactivated sword. "I'm not alone."

Rick, Alex, Zack, Amy, Judy, Jeff, Mr. Shimizu, and even a powerless Pete all appear from their hiding places in the rubble. "My friends are not as strong as me, but they were able to use The Source of all things to slow you down enough for me to finish this."

Yabechun feebly grabs at the protruding blade, unable to remove it.

I raise his blade to end this.

He lets out a weak, "I did all of this for you," unable take a full breath.

I want more than anything to end his miserable life, but in that moment, I pause with the blade ready to deliver the final blow.

"I gave up my peace for all of you." A single tear drips from his eye in his final moment.

Now I understand. A man that has been alive for over ten thousand years would have discovered the peace within The Source of all things long ago. Why has he never used the powers gained from that knowledge? Because he had to be the one to accept the darkness of this world. He gave up peace the day humanity discovered the power of God. When humanity first used nuclear weapons he was there at the epicenter. As much as I hate what he has done, without him the world would have ended long ago by our flawed mortal hands.

I lower the blade. "You're afraid to be left alone on a dead planet, waiting for the sun to consume you."

Yabechun nods his head, showing the long repressed human side of him.

Zack pleads, "What are you doing?"

The sound of helicopters begins to echo not far away.

Deactivating the weapon in my hand, I say, "I'm forgiving him."

Rick says, "Even after all the shit you said he did. After everything we just watched him do. He's too dangerous to be left alive."

I deactivate the blade protruding through his chest, returning it to my hand. "Take your necessary evil from Earth. Have your great human empire away from us."

The wound in his chest closes as he stands back up. I have no fear in this moment, though my friends back away.

Yabechun blinks away the water in his eyes. "Are you sure you want to remain on a doomed planet? This is humanity's only chance at galactic expansion."

I feel Amy's gentle touch on my shoulder as she stands behind me. "I'm sure."

Three Blackhawk helicopters land as three large soldiers in advance battle armor point their guns at us. While other military personal move to secure the dead Anunnaki monster. Yabechun waves away his armored personnel. "Were done here."

I leave the Ruined city with those closest to me. Limping just a little bit from my tumbles. Rick takes one of my arms to help me walk. While Zack collects the head of a marble statue.

Amy's father asks, "Well…now what?"

"I'm honestly not sure, Jeff." I look at his daughter as she continues to hold my hand. "And I've never been happier."

<hr>

I have made the long trek in my barely functioning vehicle across this country to Washington DC, passing through the battlegrounds the alien invaders left behind. The path is so random. One city in ruins while another carries on as if it's just another day. Reminds me of the untouched villages in Vietnam. I remember a village that did not care which army was there, just continued with their lives. If memory serves me correctly, they got hit with Agent Orange.

At my destination, I knock on the door of my recently widowed sister-in-law. I hear the crying of a baby on the other side of the door. My nephew's wife opens the door in a large T-shirt and sweatpants with a crying baby in her arms.

"Who the hel…?" She sees me. "Robert Kane? What are you doing here?"

"Just stopping by. Has Austin shipped out yet?"

She tries to soothe her baby. "No, he's packing right now."

"Good, I have something for him." I walk past her, inviting myself in. "What's that one's name?"

The baby finally stops crying.

"Oh, this is Billy."

"That's a fine name." No doubt named after William.

I find my nephew packing up his things before he ships out for a war across the stars. "Austin, are you too old to give your uncle a hug."

He obliges me unwillingly, no doubt uncomfortable by my smell. In my defense, I've been sleeping outside in various war-torn cities to get here.

"What's up, Uncle Rob?" He returns to packing. "It's too late to talk me out of this. I've already completed Basic."

"I have something for you before your journey. With John already across the galaxy and Barry's dead"—I take out an old Colt .45 Peacemaker with an ivory handle and a silver cross engraved in it, wrapped in its holster leather holster—"this falls to you."

Austin cautiously takes the pistol. "How did you get this back?"

"This pistol was used by Sinner Cain to kill his father Johnathan for control of a gang of outlaws in 1881. He used it to carve a bloody path across the West until the turn of the century when it fell to his son, your great-grandfather Jack Kane. This pistol remained at his side through two world wars. When it was given to your father during the Vietnam War, it was on him until he died holding the line in San Diego against an alien invasion. Now it belongs to you.

Use it to protect yourself as you go to fight this war beyond Earth. For you hold Judgement in your hand."

Austin holds the gun, feeling the weight of his ancestors. He can now become a true Kane. I hope he becomes a better man than me, but no matter what, he will become a killer.

TO BE CONTINUED

Dear Readers,

Thank you for taking the time to read this story. As well as a special thank you to my friends and family that support me in telling throughout the writing process. I hope you will all join me as we slowly close in on The End of Earth.

END OF EARTH

Luke Eidenschink

ABOUT THE AUTHOR

Matt Simons carried the story that would one day become The End of Earth around in his head ever since he was a little kid. The story morphed and evolved through the years, eventually becoming what it is now. All it took was a global pandemic and being trapped in quarantine to start really writing it.

A man with a sense of humor that does not exclude himself, Matt Simons is known among friends and family by his nickname, Nightstand, which he earned while carrying a nightstand down three flights of stairs and across two blocks before realizing it was nearly killing him because it was full of weights. The heavy lesson learned: check the contents of what you will carry around before lifting it.

Let's connect on social media!
Instagram: https://www.instagram.com/nightstand_matt/
Twitter: Nightstand Matt at
https://twitter.com/MattSim55879370

www.ingramcontent.com/pod-product-compliance
Lightning Source LLC
Chambersburg PA
CBHW030822210726
48290CB00002B/709